HOW MUCH SHOULD A GOOD FRIEND DO?

Katie slipped downstairs to check on Shawnie, who was hiding out in her basement.

"Hi," Shawnie said brightly. "Did I miss anything major at school today?"

"No," Katie assured her. "Just the same old stuff."

"I got lucky," Shawnie bragged. "I heard your mom make a phone call to set up an interview and then go out, so I got to go upstairs and watch soap operas for almost two hours."

"That's good," Katie said halfheartedly. She knew that she should be glad that Shawnie hadn't been stuck in the dark basement all day without even a bathroom, but she felt depressed instead. Shawnie seemed incredibly happy, living in a dark basement and laughing over each report of her parents' misery. Nothing was going right for Katie, and as much as she hated to admit it even to herself, it was all because of Shawnie. No matter how hard she tried not to doubt Shawnie's word, things were beginning to stack up against her. Who was really telling the truth, anyway? Shawnie? Or Tony and Mandy and even Mr. and Mrs. Pendergast?

THE FABULOUS FIVE

The Runaway Crisis

BETSY HAYNES

A BANTAM SKYLARK BOOK®
NEW YORK · TORONTO · LONDON · SYDNEY · AUCKLAND

RL 5, IL age 009-012

THE RUNAWAY CRISIS

A Bantam Skylark Book / May 1989

Skylark Books is a registered trademark of Bantam Books, a division of Bantam Doubleday Dell Publishing Group, Inc. Registered in U.S. Patent and Trademark Office and elsewhere.

ISBN 0-553-15719-1

Published simultaneously in the United States and Canada

Bantam Books are published by Bantam Books, a division of Bantam Doubleday Dell Publishing Group, Inc. Its trademark, consisting of the words "Bantam Books" and the portrayal of a rooster, is Registered in U.S. Patent and Trademark Office and in other countries. Marca Registrada. Bantam Books, 666 Fifth Avenue, New York, New York 10103.

PRINTED IN THE UNITED STATES OF AMERICA

CW   0 9 8 7 6 5 4 3 2 1

For Mrs. Paula Karl's seventh-grade reading classes in Colleyville Middle School, Colleyville, Texas.

CHAPTER

1

Katie Shannon had just reached the spot at the fence where The Fabulous Five met every morning before school when Beth Barry came running up. "You'll never guess what I just saw in the girls' bathroom!" she shouted.

Katie exchanged shrugs with Christie Winchell, Melanie Edwards, and Jana Morgan.

"Boys?" Melanie asked slyly, and the others laughed.

"No, silly," said Beth. "It was Shawnie Pendergast. She had one foot propped up on the sink and she was *shaving her legs!* Right here at school. Can you believe it?"

Jana made a face. "Why on earth would she do a thing like that?"

1

"I know," Katie said quietly. "She probably can't do it at home. Her parents are *really* strict. She's been talking to me about it a lot lately."

"What's she been saying?" asked Christie.

Katie hesitated. She didn't want to betray a confidence, but Shawnie hadn't asked her not to tell. Besides, she felt sorry for Shawnie and knew her best friends would sympathize, too, if they understood the situation.

"She says her parents don't allow her to go out much on weekends or to do very many things most seventh-graders get to do. In fact, a few days ago when Miss Dickinson assigned us to write bumper stickers for English Lit class that criticized something we felt was wrong with the world, Shawnie's sticker said, 'Empty the nation's prisons. Let your kid out of the house once in a while.'"

"Gosh, that's awful," said Melanie.

"She also told me that no matter what she asks her parents for permission to do, they automatically refuse," Katie went on, "and she has to sneak around to do almost anything."

"That's pretty drastic," said Melanie. "To look at her, you'd think that she has everything going for her. I mean, she's tall and blond with a gorgeous figure. And she looks more like a ninth-grader than a seventh-grader. I've always thought she was lucky."

"Have you met her parents?" Jana asked Katie.

"No. According to Shawnie, they're busy all the time. She said that they're so busy that their conversation with her consists mostly of one short word, NO."

"Poor kid," said Beth. "How does she stand it?"

"Maybe we should be extra nice to her," offered Christie. "Do you think she'd like to go to Bumpers with us after school?"

"Do you think her parents would *let* her?" chimed in Beth.

"Come to think of it, I don't remember seeing her there very often," added Melanie.

"At least we can ask," said Katie. "I have English Lit with her. I'll talk to her then."

When the bell rang and she was heading for her classes, Katie was glad she had told her friends about Shawnie's problems. Even though the five of them had totally different personalities, they could all be counted on when someone needed help. Katie knew that her own strong point was her sense of fairness, and it hurt her to think that someone as nice as Shawnie was being treated unfairly by her parents.

"I'd love to go to Bumpers with you and your friends," Shawnie said when Katie stopped her outside the door of their English classroom later in the day. "I'll just have to watch the time and make sure I get home before my parents. I'm supposed to go straight home and do my homework, but if I'm careful, they'll never know the difference."

Katie cringed. As sorry as she felt for Shawnie, she wasn't comfortable with sneaking around. "Why don't

4 THE FABULOUS FIVE

you call your mom and clear it with her? Maybe she'll
say it's okay."

"And maybe she won't, which is more likely. Then
I'd be dead. She'd find out for sure if I went anyway
after she had said her favorite word—NO. Don't
worry," Shawnie added cheerfully. "I can handle it.
I've done it lots of times before."

When Katie got to her locker after school, Tony Calcaterra was leaning against it, grinning at her as she
approached.

"How about going to Bumpers with me?" he offered. "I'll buy you a Coke."

"It's a criminal offense to bribe a judge!" she re-
torted, but she couldn't fight down the smile that
crossed her face or the tingly feeling that she always
got when she was near Tony.

"Oh, so you've heard about it already, huh?"

"Heard about what?" Katie asked in surprise.

Tony grinned proudly. "That I have to go before
Teen Court again this week."

"Of course not. We never know what cases we're
going to get until the court session starts. That way we
don't make up our minds before we hear the evidence,"
said Katie. She put her hands on her hips and gave him
an exasperated look. "What did you do this time?"

"If you're not supposed to hear about your cases
ahead of time, then I guess I shouldn't tell you about
it, should I?"

Katie sighed and shook her head in disbelief. Tony
was terrifically handsome with dark hair and sparkling

eyes, but he was also terribly macho. What was worse, he was constantly being brought before Wakeman Junior High's Teen Court, where she was a student judge, for breaking school rules. She swallowed a giggle as she remembered the last time when she had had to sentence him to removing graffiti from all over the school for spray-painting "T.C. + K.S." on the outside wall of the gym. She couldn't imagine what he had gotten himself into this time.

It was obvious that Tony had a crush on her. He had been asking her out at least once a week ever since she helped him petition the school to change the dress code rule that said boys couldn't wear earrings. In many ways he was the exact opposite of what she liked in a boy, but in other ways she admired him. He certainly stuck up for what he believed in, and even though their petition had been refused, he had respected the rule and obeyed it.

So far, though, Katie hadn't made up her mind if she wanted Tony for a boyfriend or not, and she had turned him down every time he had asked her for a date. Still, she thought, he made her heart beat like crazy and maybe going to Bumpers with him wouldn't be such a bad idea . . . just this once. "If I say yes, will you carry my books?" she teased.

"Load me down, Your Honor," Tony said with a wide smile. He held out his arms to receive them.

Laughing, Katie began pulling books out of her locker and piling them on Tony's outstretched arms until he could barely see over the top.

"On second thought," she said, standing back and

surveying him thoughtfully, "if I let you carry all of them now, how will I get them back to school in the morning?"

He winked at her over the top of her English Lit book. Then he wobbled slightly as if his knees were buckling under the weight and said in a weak, raspy voice, "I'm always at your service, ma'am."

"Hi, Katie. Are you ready to go to Bumpers?"

Katie jumped to attention at the sound of Shawnie's voice. How could she have forgotten that she had invited Shawnie to go to Bumpers with The Fabulous Five? Especially since she had extended the invitation herself?

"Darn you, Tony Calcaterra," she muttered too low for him to hear. "I can't *think* when you're around me.

"I'll be with you in a minute, Shawnie," she said, and turned back to Tony.

"What was that all about?" he asked from behind the stack of books.

Katie was relieved to see that Shawnie had moved on down the hall toward Beth, who was closing her locker.

"I can't go to Bumpers with you today," Katie said, and began retrieving books from the stack on Tony's arms and putting them back into her locker. "I totally forgot that Shawnie was going with my friends and me. If it were just The Fabulous Five I was going with, it would be different. But I'm the one who asked her to come along."

Tony frowned and looked toward Shawnie.

"She has a lot of problems at home," said Katie.

He grinned at her again. "And Her Honor Katie Shannon, champion of justice, is coming to her rescue. Is that it?"

"Don't be mean," she said. "You're just mad because she wouldn't sign your earring petition. Anyway, I'll go to Bumpers with you tomorrow . . . if you still want to."

"Of course I'll still want to," he said, "but don't get too carried away trying to help Shawnie. I went to school with her at Copper Beach, and there are a lot of things about her that you don't know."

They said good-bye, and Katie watched him trot off down the hall to join Bill Soliday and Keith Masterson at the drinking fountain. For a moment she stood there puzzling over his remark about Shawnie. Was it just sour grapes because she wouldn't sign his earring petition? Or was there really something about Shawnie that she needed to know?

CHAPTER

2

"Oh, rats! I just realized that I didn't wear my watch today," said Shawnie as the six of them left the school together. Looking straight at Katie, she said, "I need to be home before five. Would you keep me posted on how late it's getting?"

"Sure. It is now three twenty-seven post meridiem," Katie said dramatically.

"Post what?" asked Melanie.

"Post meridiem," repeated Katie. "You know, p.m., afternoon. It's Latin."

"Wow!" said Shawnie. "I'm impressed. Post meridiem, huh?"

Everybody laughed, and Katie was glad. It seemed to clear the tension out of the air. When she had told her friends that Shawnie was going to sneak around to go to Bumpers with them, no one had been comfortable with the idea. Still, no one had wanted to tell her that she couldn't go, either.

By the time they made their way through the crowd in Bumpers and found a table, Shawnie was positively glowing.

"I just love it here," she said, sweeping her arm to take in the entire fast food restaurant that was the junior high hangout. "Whoever it was who thought of salvaging old bumper cars from an amusement park ride, fixing them up, and then using them to decorate this place was a genius."

They had barely gotten seated when Christie jumped up again. "I see Jon over there," she said. "I have to talk to him a minute. Save my seat."

"I don't see Randy anywhere," said Jana, frowning.

"I see *tons* of cute boys," Melanie said in a breathless voice. "I think I'm just going to sit back and feast my eyes."

The last thing Katie wanted to do was act as boy crazy as Melanie. She didn't even want anyone to think she liked Tony the way Jana wanted everybody to know about Randy and Christie was so public about her feelings for Jon. Still, she wondered if Tony had come to Bumpers after she had changed her mind about coming with him. Looking around as casually as she could, she spotted him across the room. He was sitting in a booth with several seventh-grade football players, and he noticed her at almost the same instant.

But instead of smiling, he frowned in Shawnie's direction and shook his head.

She looked away abruptly. What's the matter with him? she wondered. He's acting as if Shawnie has something contagious.

"So, are you looking for anyone special?" Beth asked Shawnie.

Shawnie dropped her eyes. "It wouldn't do any good if I were," she said sadly. "My parents won't let me date."

"Not at *all*?" Melanie asked. "I mean not for special occasions such as school dances?"

"Nope," said Shawnie. "Not . . . at . . . all." Then she grinned sheepishly and said, "I had a boyfriend in sixth grade, but my parents didn't know it. All we could do was eat lunch together and walk around together in the halls. Some romance, huh?"

"I hate to say this," said Beth, "but your parents don't seem to be up with the times. Have you tried to talk to them and tell them about what's *normal* for somebody your age? Maybe they just don't understand."

Shawnie sighed. "They understand. And yes, I've tried to talk to them. They just want things their way, and there's nothing I can do about it."

Shawnie didn't say anything for a while after that. She just sat there looking sad, and Katie wondered if she was thinking about all the freedom The Fabulous Five had and wishing she could have just a little of it for herself.

"Hey, it's *now* four oh three," said Katie. She was

hoping to cheer Shawnie up and get her into some conversation.

"Post meridiem?" Shawnie asked brightly.

"You've got it," said Katie.

"Thanks. I've got approximately twenty minutes before I have to leave. That will give me enough time before my mom gets home from work to spread a bunch of papers around on the kitchen table to look like I've been doing my homework." Then laughing and shaking her head so that her blond hair bounced on her shoulders, she added, "My mom worships homework!"

"Would she let you come over to my house to do homework sometime?" asked Katie. "I mean, it wouldn't be very exciting, but it would get you out of the house."

Shawnie's eyes brightened. "I'd *love* it!" she said so dramatically that Katie thought she sounded like Beth. "It might take some plotting, though. You know. Your mother calling my mother or something. But it's worth a try."

"Great," said Katie. "I'll ask my mom, but I'm sure she'll say yes."

When Shawnie left at 4:27, Katie looked nervously at her friends and said, "I hope she gets home in time and doesn't get caught."

"Me, too," said Melanie. "But I also hope we don't get into trouble if she does."

"Yeah," said Christie, who had come back to the table by then. "I'd be careful if I were you, Katie. I like Shawnie and feel sorry for her, but we don't know that much about her. Who knows what kind of trouble she could stir up."

"Come on, guys," said Katie. She couldn't remember when she had been so annoyed with her friends. "Are you just going to sit there and let her go down the tubes because you don't know her that well? I'm not planning to do anything *major*. I'm just going to invite her over to do homework."

"Sorry," said Jana, but there was still an edge in her voice. "We didn't mean to come off sounding like villains."

"We just think you should be careful," offered Beth.

The crowd was starting to thin out as kids drifted out the door and headed for home. Katie said good-bye to the rest of The Fabulous Five and started down the street leading to her neighborhood.

"Hey, Katie. Wait up."

She would have recognized the voice anywhere. It was Tony, and when she turned to look at him, he was loping toward her.

"Well, Your Honor," he said playfully. "Did you accomplish your mission and rescue Shawnie Pendergast?"

Katie frowned. "What do you have against her?"

"Nothing. Honest." Tony put his arms up to protest his innocence. "I guess she's just not my type."

"But you said that there were things about her that I didn't know. What did you mean by that?"

"Save the cross-examination for court," he teased. "I'll see you at school tomorrow, and don't forget that we have a date for Bumpers. Okay?"

Tony was smiling his irresistible smile, and Katie nodded. "Okay," she said, and smiled back. Still, after he was gone, she couldn't help wondering if he had changed the subject because he wanted to talk about their date for Bumpers after school tomorrow or because he didn't want to talk about Shawnie.

CHAPTER

3

*T*he first thing Katie did when she got home from school was dump her books on the kitchen table, grab a nectarine out of the bowl of fruit on the counter, and head for her mother's office.

Wilma Shannon, who insisted on being called Willie, was a freelance writer. Ever since Katie's father died, Willie had earned a living for the two of them doing articles for newspapers and magazines. Often those articles were about causes that Willie cared about and that she wanted people to get involved with such as the women's movement and world peace. Katie's friends sometimes kidded her about being a chip off the old block, but she didn't mind. She had causes she believed in, too, and right now one of them was Shawnie Pendergast.

"Hi," she called brightly as she stuck her head into the bedroom that Willie had converted into an office. "Whoops!" she said, and ducked out again when she saw her mother sitting before the blue eye of her secondhand computer and gazing into the distance. It had taken some doing, but her mother had finally convinced her that she was working her hardest when she was staring off into space.

"It's okay," Willie called back. "I'm almost finished anyway. Libber and I just can't get this article to come out right. We need a break."

Katie chuckled and strolled into the room. Taking a bite of her nectarine, she stroked Libber, the stray yellow cat they had taken in months ago, who liked to curl up around the back of the warm and softly purring computer while her mother worked on her articles.

"I can tell that Libber needs a break," Katie joked. "She looks exhausted. What's your article about, anyway?"

"Hunger," said Willie. "Did you know that in this city alone hundreds of people go to bed hungry every night? They sleep on park benches, in vacant buildings, under bridges. And they're not just adults. Lots of them are children."

Katie let out a low whistle, but before she could say anything, her mother went on, her voice rising passionately, "And those are just the ones the authorities know about. There's no telling how many more there are. It's a *disgrace*."

"Why are you having such a hard time writing about it?"asked Katie. "It's obvious you care a lot."

"Nobody's doing anything new that I can build an article on," Willie said, sounding exasperated. "I mean, there are soup kitchens and collection points where people can drop off donations, but that's old news. Those have been around for a long time. What I need is something different that will grab people's attention and make them want to help out."

Katie shrugged sympathetically. "I haven't heard of anything around good old Wacko Junior High."

Willie smiled and shut off her computer. "So what *is* going on at good old Wacko? Anything worth talking about?"

"Well, sort of," Katie began. She knew that hunger was a lot bigger problem than one girl's troubles with her parents, but she didn't want to let Shawnie down. "I have a new friend. Her name is Shawnie Pendergast, and her parents are *unreal*. They won't let her do *anything*."

Katie told her mother the whole story of Shawnie and her parents, leaving out only the parts about Shawnie's sneaking around. As liberal as Willie was about some things, Katie wasn't sure how she would feel about that.

"Anyway," she concluded, "I'd like to invite Shawnie over sometime. We'd have to make it a homework session, and you'd have to call Shawnie's mother and convince her that we were really going to study before she'd give Shawnie permission, but it would be worth it. She needs to get out of the house."

Willie sighed deeply. "Wow," she said. "It's hard to believe anyone could be that strict."

"Will you do it?" Katie asked.

"Sure," said Willie, giving her daughter a hug. "You decide when you want her to come, and I'll take care of the rest."

Katie didn't know why she felt so relieved. She had known Willie would help once she understood the situation. That was just the kind of person her mother was.

When Katie got to school the next morning, she went inside the building to look for Shawnie instead of meeting her friends outside at the fence. She found her at the drinking fountain beside the office.

She had meant to ask Shawnie immediately if she had gotten home from Bumpers before her mother returned from work, but instead her mouth dropped open at the sight of Shawnie's gorgeous outfit.

"Like it?" asked Shawnie. Then she twirled around so that Katie could get the full effect of the deep-burgundy-colored jumper and matching beige-and-burgundy blouse. Even her lipstick matched, and her blond hair shone like spun gold in contrast to the dark color of the jumper, making her look like a magazine model.

"It's beautiful," Katie murmured, and tried not to wonder how much it had cost.

"I like it, too, but it's only a payoff," said Shawnie.

"A payoff?" Katie echoed.

"To make up for not letting me do anything or go anywhere," Shawnie said matter-of-factly. "My mom thinks that if she buys me a new outfit to wear to school every so often, it will fix everything." Then her face brightened. "At least I made it home before she did yesterday, but just barely. I hadn't even taken my coat off when I heard her car in the driveway. You wouldn't believe how fast I moved to make it look as if I'd been home for ages."

"Whoa! I'm glad you made it," said Katie. "By the way, I asked my mom about calling your mom to see if you can come over some evening. I explained that she'd have to promise your mom that we would do home-work. She said she'd be glad to."

Shawnie just looked at her for a moment, and Katie thought she saw Shawnie's eyes get misty. "Thanks a million. Your mom sounds like a real doll." Then her face lit up again and she added with a wink, "We will study, too! At least part of the time."

Katie laughed along with Shawnie, but at the same time she felt a catch in her throat. Poor Shawnie, she thought. It wasn't fair that her life was so miserable. Merely inviting Shawnie to her house once in a while wasn't going to be nearly enough. There had to be more she could do.

CHAPTER

4

At lunchtime Katie brought up the subject of Shawnie with her friends again.

"Can you believe a mother who pays off her daughter with clothes for *not* letting her do things? That's what Shawnie told me this morning that her mother does. And believe me, the new outfit she has on today looks EX . . . PEN . . . SIVE."

Melanie chuckled. "I wish my mom would pay me off for not doing something. I could use some new clothes. And there are lots of things she could pay me off for. *Not* baby-sitting Jeffy. *Not* cleaning my room. Things like that."

Everybody laughed except Katie. "This is serious. You have no idea how miserable Shawnie is."

Jana looked at Katie sympathetically. "We didn't mean to make fun of Shawnie's situation," she said. "You know us better than that, don't you?"

Katie nodded. "Sure. I guess I'm getting a little carried away. But it isn't fair, you know. Shawnie ought to have some rights, too."

"But what can any of us do about it?" asked Christie. "After all, her parents *are* her parents."

"Well, I'm going to invite her over some evening soon," Katie answered. "Shawnie said my mom would have to call her mom and say it would be a study session, though. Hey! I've got an idea! Why don't you guys come over, too? We can do our homework and then listen to tapes."

"I've got an even better idea," chirped Melanie. "Let's invite boys and make it a real party." Her grin faded immediately as Katie shot her a warning look. "Okay. Okay. I was just trying to be funny," she offered. Then she gave Katie a sly glance. "Speaking of boys, though, didn't I see you kidding around with Tony Calcaterra at your locker yesterday after school and then talking to him later outside Bumpers?"

Katie could feel her face turning red at the mention of Tony Calcaterra. What was worse, it was Melanie who had brought his name up. Katie was always calling Melanie boy crazy because she had crushes on tons of boys and flirted with every boy in sight. But now Melanie had caught Katie in the act of flirting, and it looked as if she wasn't going to let Katie off the hook.

"So? There's no law against talking to someone, is there?" Katie asked defensively.

"Speaking of law," Beth chimed in, "I'll bet she was asking him if he's done anything to land himself in Teen Court this week."

The flame in Katie's face burned hotter. Just wait until they hear that he *will* be in Teen Court this week, she thought, and then said quickly, "For your information, I was talking to him about something very important."

"Oh, sure," teased Christie. "He's probably decided to take up one of your causes."

"As a matter of fact, he has. He's interested in . . . in hunger." Katie couldn't believe the words that were tumbling out of her own mouth, but she couldn't stop them. "He wants to do something. Maybe even organize a march for hunger. Did you know that every night hundreds of people go to bed hungry in this town alone?"

"And Tony Calcaterra wants to do something about it?" Jana asked incredulously. "When did he become Mr. Concerned Citizen?"

"Since he got a major crush on Katie, apparently," said Melanie, rolling her eyes heavenward as if she could hardly believe it either. "Love does strange things to people."

"So tell us about this march for hunger," said Christie. "It sounds like a good idea."

Katie took a deep breath and tried to sort out her thoughts. Her mind had been racing ever since she had opened her mouth and told that incredible lie about Tony and the march. Half of her brain was in shock over the fact that she would do such a thing and was chewing her out for letting Tony get to her. The other half was desperately trying to figure out how to get out of the mess she had just gotten herself into.

"Well," urged Melanie. "Are you going to tell us? Or is it a deep, dark secret?"

"It's a secret," said Katie, jumping on Melanie's words. "Well, it isn't exactly a secret," she went on. "We're still working on the details. In fact, we're going to talk more about it after school today."

"You're really serious, aren't you?" said Jana, nodding her head in approval. "I mean, you're probably the only person in the world who could get Tony Calcaterra interested in doing something for humanity. I have to hand it to you, Katie. You're special."

"I agree," said Beth. "Most of us just sit back and shake our heads about things and say 'Isn't that too bad,' but you get busy and do something about it. Look at how you're trying to help Shawnie, and now this—inspiring Tony to do something besides get into trouble. You can count me in for both things. I'll come when you invite Shawnie over, and I'll join the march for hunger."

"Me, too," said Melanie.

"Me, too," echoed Christie and Jana.

"Thanks, guys," said Katie. "I always knew I could count on The Fabulous Five." But deep down in the pit of her stomach a funny feeling was growing. How was she going to get Tony to organize a march for hunger? And worse yet, persuade him that it had been his own idea?

CHAPTER

5

*K*atie spent the entire afternoon worrying about what she would say to Tony. She had never been in such a predicament in her life, and it was all because of a *boy*. Tony was macho. He was a show-off. He got into trouble constantly. He was all the things that she had never liked in a boy.

Still, she thought, doodling circles around the edge of her paper in last period English class. He treated her as if she were special. He had stood up for her when Teen Court had first started a few weeks ago, and Clarence Marshall and Joel Murphy were teasing her about her detention. He had followed the dress code rule by not wearing his earring even though his petition had failed. He had a major crush on her. And he was just about the best-looking boy in Wakeman Junior High. But that wasn't all, she mused. There was something else about him. Something she couldn't quite define that made her blush and get totally flustered every time his name came up. Something that even made her think about him at times when she should have been thinking about something else. Like now.

"Katie Shannon, I asked you a question."

Miss Dickinson's words pierced her daydream and jabbed her back to reality.

"I'm sorry, Miss Dickinson," Katie said sheepishly. "I didn't hear what you asked."

Before Miss Dickinson could answer, the bell rang. "Don't forget, class," she called instead. "Your assignment is to write a two-hundred-and-fifty-word theme on the quotation on the blackboard. It is due one week from today."

Katie frowned. She hadn't heard Miss Dickinson make the theme assignment, either. As kids streamed past her heading for the door, she hurriedly copied the quotation into her notebook.

> *If there were dreams to sell, what would you buy?*
> —Thomas Lovell Beddoes

"Fifty-yard-line seats for the Super Bowl!" Matt Zeboski shouted as he dove for the door.

"A lifetime supply of *pizza*!" roared Clarence Marshall.

Boys! thought Katie as she gathered her books and

followed the rest of the class out of the room. They were so shallow. So immature.

She was still frowning when she rounded the corner and saw Tony leaning against her locker again. He was watching her approach with the same confident smile he had had the day before. But try as she might to stay cool, she felt a warm glow as a smile spread over her own face.

"Hi, there, Your Honor. Are we still on for today?"

"Sure. I just have to get my jacket out of my locker," Katie said, but the instant the words were out, she started to worry. Had her voice been two octaves higher than normal? Had she sounded uptight instead of casual?

She put the books from her afternoon classes into her locker, keeping out only her notebook, and slipped on her jacket.

Tony was grinning slyly as they started off down the hall. "Since you only have your notebook and I have two *big, heavy books*, maybe today you should help me out," he reasoned. Then, before she could answer, he flipped his history book toward her.

Laughing, she reached out with her left hand and caught it.

"Not a bad catch for a judge," he teased.

As they left the school ground, Katie hugged her notebook and Tony's history book to her chest and began to panic. She had to talk to him about organizing a march for the hungry, and she had to do it today before one of her friends got the chance to say something to him about it. One of them might, too, especially Christie or Jana. They might stop him in the hall and tell him how much they liked his idea. Her face turned red just thinking about how confused he would be. He might even say something smart, such as, "Yeah, let's march on down to the cafeteria and see what's on for today."

Bumpers was packed, as usual, and Tony steered her through the crowd as they looked for somewhere to sit. Katie waved to the rest of The Fabulous Five in a booth near the front, and Tony gave high fives to Mark Peters and Bill Soliday as they passed their table. Luckily they had just stopped beside an orange bumper car when two eighth-graders vacated it, and they jumped in before someone else could get it.

Katie fidgeted nervously and took long drinks of the soda Tony brought back from the order counter.

"Are you always this quiet when you're alone with a guy?" Tony asked.

"No . . . I mean, yes . . . I mean, I was just wondering something," stammered Katie.

"Something about me?"

Katie nodded. "How do you feel about hunger?" she blurted.

Tony was looking at her as if she had just asked if he had ever walked on the moon. She knew her face was blazing. Why couldn't she keep a cool head and talk like a normal person when she was around him?

"Well, it's a constant struggle," he said with mock seriousness. "I fight it with at least three meals a day and a bunch of snacks in between." Then he gave her a puzzled look. "What do you mean, how do I feel about hunger?"

"I'm very concerned about it," she said over the hammering of her heart. "You see, my mother is writing an article about hunger, and she says that hundreds of people right here in this city go to bed hungry every night. She also said that nothing new is being done about it, and I think that's awful. Don't you?"

"Well . . . sure. I guess so," said Tony. "But what does that have to do with me?"

"I just thought that if you were concerned, you might want to do something about it. That's all."

The puzzled expression was still on Tony's face. "Like what?"

Katie took a deep breath and charged on. She couldn't stop now. "Oh, something fun . . . such as getting all the kids at Wacko to put on a march for hunger."

"Who, *me*?" Tony asked incredulously.

"Sure. Why not?" said Katie. "I'd be glad to help."

Tony drank his soda in silence for a moment, and Katie could practically see little wheels turning in his brain as he thought over the idea. She chewed the end of her straw, not daring to wonder what she would do if he said no.

"You'd help, huh?" he asked, and then without giving her time to answer he went on, "I know what you're doing. You're trying to make me look good for Teen Court and also for Mr. Bell and the school board so that when the petition comes up again to allow earrings at school, they'll think I'm a great person instead of a juvenile delinquent. Is that it?"

Katie stared at him. She hadn't thought about it that way, but it wasn't such a bad idea. "It wouldn't hurt," she offered. "But also it could really help a lot of people. And I honestly would help get it organized. I promise." Gulping hard, she said, "We could work on it *together*."

Tony cocked one eyebrow and looked at her appraisingly. "Okay," he said. "You've got a deal."

CHAPTER

6

*K*atie could hardly wait to get home and tell her mother about the march for hunger, and she sprinted all the way to her front door after she said good-bye to Tony. She had been trying for a long time to think of a way to bring up the subject of Tony to her mother. Not that Willie would mind that she was interested in a boy. It was just that she hadn't been sure if she really was interested—until now.

She and Tony had talked a little bit more about how to get the march organized before they left Bumpers, and she had suggested that they go together to talk to Mr. Bell tomorrow morning before school. They would have to get the principal's permission in order to get the school involved.

"Katie? Is that you?" her mother called as the front door slammed behind her.

"Yeah, Mom."

Willie appeared in the living room doorway. "Your friend Shawnie Pendergast called a few minutes ago. She wants you to call her back as soon as possible."

"Is something wrong?" asked Katie.

"I honestly don't know, honey," her mother replied. "But she sounded extremely anxious to talk to you."

"Thanks," said Katie. "I'll call her right now."

The phone had barely finished its first ring when Shawnie answered. "I'm so glad you called," she whispered when she found out it was Katie. "I've just got to get out of this house. Could your mom call my mom about coming over to study tonight? Believe me, it's an emergency."

"An emergency?" Katie whispered back. "What kind of emergency?"

"I can't talk now."

"Okay, Shawnie," Katie said. "You know I want to help. Hang on while I ask her."

"I have to go. I think I hear one of my parents coming. Have your mother call here if it's okay."

Katie slammed down the receiver and raced to find her mother. "Mom," Katie began in a shaky voice. "Shawnie wants to come over tonight. She says it's an emergency. Will you call her parents?"

Willie looked up from her desk and frowned. "Did she say what sort of emergency?"

"No. She was even whispering so that no one would

know she was on the phone. Then she said she had to hang up because she thought someone was coming."

Her mother sighed. "Gosh, Katie, I don't know. It sounds as if we might be interfering in something that isn't any of our business."

"Mom, please. She's desperate," said Katie. "Besides, we can talk to her and find out what the problem is once she's here . . . if they'll even let her come."

Willie considered the situation for another moment while Katie stood by her desk and pleaded with her eyes. "Well," she said at last, "all we can do is try."

Katie bounced nervously from foot to foot while her mother made the call. "Hello, Mrs. Pendergast? . . . I'm Willie Shannon, Katie's mother, and Katie would like for Shawnie to come over here for a little while this evening so that the girls can work on some homework together. Would that be all right with you? . . . It would?" Willie turned and gave Katie a wide-eyed shrug. "Wonderful . . . Why not drop her off around six-thirty? . . . Great. Good-bye."

Katie grabbed her mother around the waist. "I can't believe it!" she shouted. "She said yes? Just like that?"

"Just like that," said Willie. "Actually, she was formal and businesslike, but she sounded reasonably nice over the phone. Maybe things aren't so bad after all."

"I hope not," said Katie.

At exactly six-thirty a dark car pulled up beside the curb, and Shawnie Pendergast got out carrying a load of books and hurried to the door. Katie had been watching for her for ten minutes and wondering what kind of situation it was that Shawnie had called an emergency. Willie had suggested that Katie talk to Shawnie about it and then call her in if it was necessary. "There's no use making this thing any bigger than it is," Willie had commented, and Katie had agreed.

"Come on in," said Katie as she opened the door for Shawnie.

"Thanks," said Shawnie. Taking a deep breath and then letting it out slowly, she leaned back against the closed door as if she had just made it to safety. "I really appreciate this."

"Put your books down and take off your jacket, and I'll introduce you to my mom," said Katie. A moment later in Willie's office Katie made the introductions.

"It's nice to meet you, Shawnie. I'm glad you could come over," said Willie, standing up from her desk and extending her hand to Shawnie.

"Thanks, Mrs. Shannon. It's nice to meet you, too. I really appreciate your calling my mom."

"Anytime, Shawnie. I know it can be a big help to study together."

Katie was thinking what a good actress her mother was, not letting on that she knew Shawnie had problems at home, when she noticed a flicker of concern in Willie's eyes. She followed her mother's gaze and saw a large, dark bruise on Shawnie's right arm just above her elbow.

Shawnie must have noticed Willie's gaze, too, because she shrugged and pulled the sleeve of her sweater over the bruise. "You wouldn't believe how clumsy I am," she said with an embarrassed little laugh. "I walked right into my closet door."

Katie felt a knot forming in the pit of her stomach. There was no way she could believe that Shawnie had walked into her closet door. Had one of her parents hit her? Was that what her emergency had been? Katie blinked and looked at Shawnie again as if she were seeing her for the very first time. Tall, pretty Shawnie with the long blond hair and the gorgeous wardrobe who had seemed at first to have everything going for her. Was it possible that things were as bad for her at home as they looked?

Libber chose that moment to unwind herself from around the back of Willie's computer. She walked across the manuscript pages straight toward Shawnie, stopping only to yawn and stretch before reaching out a paw and looking pleadingly at Katie's friend.

"Look! She likes me," cried Shawnie. "Is it okay if I pick her up?"

Katie nodded and chuckled. "You'd better or she'll pester you all evening. Her name is Libber because she's a totally liberated woman."

Shawnie picked up Libber and held her close, nuzzling her soft, yellow hair. "She sounds like a jet plane on takeoff," remarked Shawnie as she gently placed Libber on the floor. "I wish I could have a cat. One just like Libber. But we have a rule at our house. *No pets*."

· "We'd better get started on our homework," said Katie, feeling uneasy again. "But first, let's see what we can dig up to snack on."

"See you later, girls," said Willie as the two left her office with Libber padding along behind them.

"We have another rule at our house," said Shawnie, watching Katie fill a large bowl with chips and pop two cans of soda. *"No snacks in between meals. It's grim."*

"Why are your parents so strict?" asked Katie. "I mean, do they tell you any reasons?"

"Sure. They tell me their reasons all the time. They're doing what's best for me." She said the last words slowly and deliberately as if echoing the way her parents spoke.

Katie took a deep breath. There was one more question she had to ask. It took all her effort to keep her eyes away from the bruise on Shawnie's arm as she said, "You haven't told me yet what your emergency was."

Shawnie's eyes clouded, and she chewed her bottom lip as she considered her response. "I'd rather not talk about it right now. Okay?"

"Are you sure?" Katie insisted. "You know I want to help, and sometimes just talking about something can make you feel better."

"Thanks," said Shawnie. "You're a super friend, but believe me, talking about this is definitely not something I want to do. Besides," she added brightly, "we have a theme to write for Miss Dickinson. We'd better get started."

Katie nodded and opened her notebook to the hastily copied quotation.

If there were dreams to sell, what would you buy?

Wow, thought Katie. Any other time the theme would have been a breeze. Her dreams had always been the causes she believed in, such as justice, equality, even her new one, helping the hungry. They still were, of course, and she knew that she would probably write her theme on one of them. But now she had a new dream, a new cause. Brushing tears out of her eyes, she glanced at Shawnie, who sat with her head bent over her own notebook and with Libber curled contentedly in her lap.

I'm going to do something to help Shawnie Pendergast, Katie vowed silently. She didn't know what that something would turn out to be, but no matter how hard it was, she would do it because Shawnie needed her help and she had no one else to turn to.

CHAPTER

7

*W*alking to school the next morning, Katie thought back over the evening. Shawnie had kept her lips sealed about the emergency at home even though Katie had mentioned her willingness to help several times. She had even hinted that her mother would help, too. After Shawnie's parents picked her up at nine-thirty, Katie had a long conversation with Willie.

"I feel so sorry for her," Katie began. "She must be too scared to tell me what happened. What are we going to do?"

"We can't do much to help her as long as she won't talk about the problem," Willie had said. "But not only that, we have to be awfully careful about butting into another family's business. For all we know, things may not be nearly the way they seem."

Katie knew her mother was right about not being able to help Shawnie if she didn't want them to, and also about being careful. But Katie had no doubt in her own mind about how bad things were for Shawnie, and Willie's words did nothing to alter her determination to help her new friend.

Finally she had told Willie about Tony and the march for hunger. "Now you'll have something to write about," she said proudly. "Tony and I are going to make this the best march ever. We'll get all the students in Wakeman Junior High involved and ask them to get pledges of a certain amount of money for every mile they walk from all their friends and relatives."

Willie had reacted just the way Katie had hoped she would. "Katie, that's terrific!" she said, giving her daughter a hug. "I am so proud of you. You know," she added thoughtfully, "sometimes when I'm out working on stories for the paper, I see whole families who have nowhere to live just sitting on park benches waiting for the shelters to open up and take them in. It reminds me of how lucky you and I are."

Katie nodded. She had seen the street people, too. It wasn't fair, she thought. Everyone should have somewhere to live and enough to eat.

"Have you decided who will get the money you collect?"

Katie shook her head. "I was going to ask you for suggestions since you already know so much about the subject."

"Well, there's the county food bank that gives bags of groceries to families who need them," said Willie, "and there are two organizations who serve meals to the street people every day. They're always in need of donations."

"Great," said Katie. "We'll get every single kid in Wacko to sign up, and then we'll collect as much as we possibly can."

Her mother smiled. "I'll tell you what. You give me all the information about your march, and I'll call all three organizations to tell them your plans and then write the first article about it tonight for the newspaper. The publicity should help you get more and bigger pledges from people around town."

Now, on the way to school, Katie was feeling more proud than ever about the march for hunger. Still, she knew that there was one thing that she hadn't talked to her mother about, and that was her mixed feelings for Tony. It was still true that part of her disliked a lot of things about him, but it was also true that the other part of her was starting to like him more than ever, and little tingly feelings danced up her spine when she came in sight of the school and saw him waiting for her beside the gate.

"Hi, there, Your Honor," he called as she got near. "Are you ready to talk to the prince?"

"The 'prince'?" asked Katie.

Tony laughed. "That's short for 'principal.'" Then when he saw her wrinkle her nose, he added, "Cornball, huh?"

"You've got it," Katie said, but she couldn't help laughing anyway.

They walked toward the building in comfortable silence until Tony said, "You know, it's funny, but the more I think about this march for hunger, the better I like the whole idea."

Katie's spirits zoomed. "You do? That's great!"

"I guess I just hadn't thought much about anything like that before. You know, that I could do something. But I think it's going to be a lot of fun. I just hope the prince . . . uh, Mr. Bell lets us go through with it."

"Me, too," admitted Katie. "My mom's going to try to get an article about it into this afternoon's paper. If he turns us down, I'll have to call her and tell her not to print it."

Miss Simone was pounding away on her typewriter when Katie and Tony entered the office, and Katie shook her head in wonder at how the secretary managed to hit the keys in spite of her long, red fingernails.

"What can I do for you two?" Miss Simone asked sharply.

Katie started to respond, but Tony stepped forward and took charge. "We'd like to speak to Mr. Bell, please."

Miss Simone stopped typing and looked over the top of her glasses at them as if she was trying to figure out what the two of them could possibly have to say to Mr. Bell. Finally she stood and said, "Just a moment. I'll see if he's available," and disappeared into his private office. A moment later she reappeared.

"Go on in. He'll see you now."

Tony and Katie exchanged thumbs-up signs and hurried into the principal's office. Katie could see that Tony was starting to get a little nervous, and she smiled to herself, speculating that the only times he had been in the principal's office before this had been because he was in trouble.

"What can I do for the two of you this morning?" Mr. Bell asked cheerfully. He was a tall, thin man with a bald spot shining through a fringe of gray hair, and he leaned back at his desk and smiled at them.

Katie decided she should take charge this time. "We would like to organize a march for hunger at Wakeman Junior High, and we thought we should get your permission before we get started."

Mr. Bell raised his eyebrows approvingly. "Well, that sounds like a fine thing to do. Tell me more about it."

For the next five minutes Katie and Tony outlined their plan. They had set a date for two weeks from Saturday, and they wanted to put an article in the school paper and posters in the halls asking students to sign up to march. The marchers would ask friends and relatives to pledge money, so much for every mile marched, which would go to the three organizations in town who fed the hungry that Willie had suggested.

"It will just be for Wacko students," Tony said cheerfully. Then blushing, he said, "I mean Wakeman Junior High students, sir."

Mr. Bell chuckled. "I've heard it called Wacko a few times, Tony," he admitted. "And I think it's a wonderful project for the school to become involved in. You have my approval. In fact, you can count on me to help any way I can. How about if I start out by pledging two dollars per mile to each of you?"

Katie and Tony exchanged wide smiles and thanked Mr. Bell at least three times as they left his office, but they waited until they were in the hall again to let out a whoop of self-congratulation.

"We did it!" cried Katie, jumping up and down.

"Hey, give me high five!" Tony shouted. Then he held his hand palm up, and Katie smacked it with her own. "This is too much," he said, shaking his head. "Tony Calcaterra, champion of the downtrodden . . . or whatever they're called. Nobody's going to believe it."

"I believe it," Katie said stubbornly.

Tony blinked in surprise. "In that case, maybe we ought to celebrate," he offered. "Would you like to go to a movie with me Friday night?"

Katie could hear her pulse pounding in her ears. This was it. The moment had come when she had to tell Tony yes or no for once and for all. She couldn't put off making a decision any longer.

"Well?" he urged.

She took a deep breath. "Yes," she answered in a tiny voice.

CHAPTER

8

Somehow being around Tony was easier once Katie
had accepted a date with him, and they spent the rest
of the time before the bell rang sitting on the front
steps together planning the march.

"We'll have to start talking it up to all our friends and
to everybody in our classes," said Tony. "And I'll bet
Mr. Bell will let us put sign-up sheets on the main bul-
letin board beside the office."

"That might not be such a good place," said Katie.
"Without someone watching, kids might sign up other
people as a joke."

Tony nodded. "Or Pee-wee Herman. Or Rambo."

"Or worse," conceded Katie.

"I've got a better idea," said Tony. "Why don't you

and I sit at a table in the cafeteria every day and collect signatures there. We could get a small table from the custodian and set it up by the cashier where everybody would see us."

"Terrific idea," said Katie. She hoped her voice sounded normal or that she didn't look fidgety. She was having a hard time sitting still now that he had not only asked her to go to a movie with him but had suggested that they have lunch together every day, too.

". . . and we can take the sign-up sheets to Bumpers after school and talk to kids on the school ground before the bell every morning," Tony was saying. His eyes were sparkling, and Katie could hear excitement growing in his voice.

A shiver ran through her. Things were moving awfully fast. She supposed she would take some flak from people such as Laura McCall and her crowd about being seen with Tony, especially after all the noise they had made when Teen Court first started. Laura had accused Katie of letting Tony off easy and giving Laura's friends tough sentences. Katie even dreaded explaining her change of heart to the rest of The Fabulous Five. They suspected, of course, but she had hoped she would have until Friday night to think of something convincing. Something that would explain why someone like herself would fall for someone like Tony. But now, if the two of them were going to be together all the time getting kids to sign up for the march, she would have to think of something quickly when she didn't even understand it herself.

When the bell rang, Katie agreed to meet Tony in

the cafeteria at noon and headed for her locker. The rest of The Fabulous Five were waiting for her in the hall.

"We saw you with Tony yesterday at Bumpers and this morning on the steps," said Beth, grinning broadly. "Did it take all that time to make plans for the march for hunger?"

"Or is it going to be a march for love?" teased Melanie.

"Okay, you guys. Knock it off. This is serious," Katie warned. She tried to sound annoyed, but she could tell by the way her friends were looking at her that she wasn't succeeding.

"So, are you really going to have the march?" asked Christie.

Katie nodded. "Tony and I talked to Mr. Bell a few minutes ago, and he thinks it's a terrific idea. We're going to have sign-up sheets in the cafeteria during lunch period and at Bumpers after school."

"*You and Tony* are going to have the sign-up sheets?" Jana asked knowingly. "How romantic!"

"I just can't believe it, Katie," said Christie, shaking her head. "You and Tony are such opposites. I mean, how can you, of all people, be organizing a march for hunger with *him*? Especially after what he did yesterday."

"What are you talking about?" Katie demanded. She swallowed hard, trying to ignore the prickly feeling on the back of her neck as she remembered his mentioning that he would be back in Teen Court this week.

"You mean you haven't heard?" asked Beth. "Wow.

Wait until you hear this. You know the girls' bathroom in the hall past the cafeteria? Well, *someone* sneaked into the custodian's office and got a sign that said: KEEP OUT—MAINTENANCE PERSONNEL AT WORK. Then that *someone* propped open the door with a bucket and hung the sign on the door, and for three whole hours nobody could go in."

"Right," interrupted Melanie. "Just think. *Three whole hours.* Some girls were so desperate that they tried to get to the bathroom at the other end of the school, and most of them ended up being late for class and getting tardy slips."

"Finally, Mr. Bartosik, the custodian, walked down the hall and noticed the sign," said Christie. "He knew that nothing was broken in there and that nobody had called the maintenance people, so he took the sign down and notified the office."

"And now I suppose everybody just assumes that Tony did it because he's in trouble so much," Katie said angrily. "Is that it?"

Beth shook her head. "No, somebody saw him carrying the sign through the halls just before the last bell rang and ratted on him."

Katie knew that her face must be turning red because she could feel steam rising from under her collar. "Oh," she mumbled, trying to hide her embarrassment by looking at the floor. "I'll see you guys later. I have to go to my locker."

She turned and scooted down the hallway before anyone could say anything else. In addition to her embarrassment, her heart was bursting. Why was Tony always getting into trouble? Couldn't he see what it did to his reputation? That it kept everyone but her from understanding what he was really like? And now this. It was the worst thing he had ever done. How could she possibly level with her friends and admit that she had a date with him for Friday night? They'll never understand, she thought. Not only that, they're *never* going to let me live this down.

In spite of all that had been happening, Katie had been keeping an eye out for Shawnie. She was going through the hall toward her first class wondering what to do about Tony when she saw Shawnie in the crowd ahead of her.

"Shawnie!" she called. When Shawnie looked back over her shoulder, Katie said, "Wait for me."

Shawnie nodded. At the next doorway she pulled away from the stream of students pushing their way along like a single wave. "Hi. Where have you been? I've been looking all over for you."

"I'll explain later. What I want to know right now is how things went when you got home last night. Is everything okay?"

"Sure," said Shawnie. "Well . . . mostly anyway. But it was worth it. Honest, it was. Thanks again for inviting me over."

Katie could only nod. She was afraid that if she spoke, Shawnie would guess from the sound of her voice how angry she was with the Pendergasts. What had they done to Shawnie when she got home last night? It couldn't have been too bad since Shawnie had said it was worth it, and Katie couldn't see any new bruises. But still!

"How often do you think your parents would let you come over?" Katie asked. "My mom would be glad to call as often as we want. Maybe we could say we're partners for a project or something, and that we need to work together every night."

"Gosh, Katie. You'd do that for me? You're the most wonderful friend I've ever had. And your mom, too. I don't know what I'd do without you." Then her face clouded. "I'll have to feel out my parents about coming over very often, though. They might get suspicious and say I couldn't do it at all. I'll have to let you know."

"You can count on me for anything," Katie assured her. Then she reached out and gave Shawnie's hand a squeeze. Shawnie smiled bravely, and Katie could see a tear shining in the corner of each eye. "Don't worry," Katie said softly. "Everything is going to be okay."

Katie decided that the moment had come to change the subject, and she spent the next couple of minutes explaining about the march for hunger. "Do you want to make some posters?" she asked after Shawnie said she thought the march was a great idea.

"Sure. I'll make some tonight after I finish my homework. And count me in for the march, too. I can't believe my parents wouldn't let me do something for charity. Especially since it's on a Saturday afternoon and won't interfere with school or homework."

When the girls parted to go to their classes, Katie was feeling a lot better about Shawnie. She knew what she had to do now: encourage Shawnie to spend every possible moment at her house. She would get the rest of The Fabulous Five involved, too. After all, they had offered to come over when she invited Shawnie. It was just that there hadn't been time last night.

Maybe Tony would help, too, she thought. He might know someone who could ask Shawnie out for Friday night and they could double. She frowned, remembering that Shawnie had said her parents wouldn't let her date. Not even for special occasions.

Then the frown deepened as she remembered another conversation, one she had had with Tony a couple of days ago. She wasn't sure he would help anyway. Hadn't he warned her against becoming too friendly with Shawnie? And said there were things about her that Katie didn't know?

CHAPTER

9

*F*or the next couple of days Katie and Tony were so busy organizing the march and conducting the sign-up that she had little time to concentrate on Shawnie. Mr. Bell kept his promise to help by inserting a notice about the march in the morning announcements that went around to every class during homeroom, and almost instantly both of them were besieged by kids wanting to sign up.

They collected two hundred and fifty signatures at the sign-up tables in the cafeteria plus others from kids who stopped them in the halls or talked to them in classes, and the newspaper sent a photographer out to shoot a picture of the two of them to run with the article Willie had written.

The only downer was the teasing Katie got from the other kids over Tony.

"How's the sign-up going?" asked Alexis Duvall, who was walking with Lisa Snow between classes the second day.

"Tony and I haven't had time to count all of them yet," Katie answered.

"You and Tony, huh?" said Lisa, raising an eyebrow. "I've heard about rehabilitating criminals, but this is too much."

"He isn't a criminal," Katie insisted angrily. "He's a very caring person, and he wants to help the hungry."

"*Sure* he does," said Alexis, and the two girls went off down the hall giggling together.

Katie fumed as she watched them go. It was going to take a lot of work on her part to convince everyone how much Tony had changed, but for now, she had other things to take care of. Making sure they got the march off to a good start, for one. And getting ready for her date with him on Friday night, for another.

Everyone in Wacko Junior High seemed to be excited about the march for hunger, including The Fabulous Five.

"I'm going to every single house in my neighborhood to get pledges," said Melanie.

"Me, too," promised Jana. "And I might even call my grandmother in Morristown, New Jersey. She could always send a check in the mail."

By the time the local newspaper was delivered Thursday evening with the article and Tony and Katie's picture in it, her confidence was soaring. Not one person she had talked to had anything negative to say about the march. It was going to be a terrific success, and she *hoped* it would convince everyone that Tony Calcaterra had changed. She cut the picture out and set it up against her dresser mirror. It was a terrific picture, especially of Tony, and she couldn't help looking at it every time she passed by.

Friday morning before the bell Katie searched for Shawnie. She felt a little guilty about not inviting Shawnie over again after all the talking she had done about wanting to help her. But the march had been taking up so much of her time that she barely had time for meals and homework. And even though she had a hard time admitting it to herself, she had gotten in more than a little daydreaming time about Tony, too. When she couldn't find her friend anywhere on the school ground, Katie looked in the girls' bathroom. Still, there was no sign of Shawnie.

She wasn't at her locker, and none of The Fabulous Five could remember seeing her when Katie asked them. By second period, when she hadn't seen Shawnie in any of the usual places between classes, Katie was convinced that she was absent.

She's probably just home with a cold or something like that, Katie decided.

Katie slipped into the media center after school for the weekly session of Teen Court. Garrett and Shane were arranging the tables end to end, and Daphne Alexandrou and Shelly Bramlett were each dragging up the last of the chairs.

Katie had been dreading today's hearings ever since Tony told her that he would be appearing before the court. Of all the weeks for him to be in trouble, she thought and frowned. *I certainly hope it won't make things awkward for our date tonight.*

When everyone was seated Miss Dickinson handed out pads of paper and pencils while Mrs. Brenner addressed the group. "We've got a fairly easy agenda this afternoon, people. We only have one case."

Easy for you to say, thought Katie.

"First, let's choose our senior judge and bailiff," Mrs. Brenner continued.

Katie slid down in her seat. She remembered all too clearly the time she had been senior judge when Tony had come before the court for violating the school dress code by wearing an earring. And then, the very next time the court met, he had been back for spray painting "T.C. + K.S." on an outside school wall. Katie wouldn't *let* Mrs. Brenner choose her for senior judge this time.

Mrs. Brenner's eyes passed over everyone, and when she came to Katie, she smiled. "I think D. J. Doyle should be senior judge this time," she said. Katie breathed a sigh of relief.

"And Katie can be bailiff."

"Yes, ma'am," Katie answered. "But I think, maybe, I ought to disqualify myself from voting," she said in a little voice. The other kids snickered and Shane Arrington buried his face in his hands. Garrett Boldt and Kaci Davis looked up at the ceiling. Katie felt her face burning and knew that she must look like a flashing red traffic light.

"All right, Katie. I understand," Mrs. Brenner said.

Great, thought Katie. Why do I let him get me into things like this? Well, it's better than having to be senior judge. I just get to lead him to the slaughter. I wonder if I'll have to take him to the gas chamber, too.

Mrs. Brenner explained the case to the court. Katie didn't see any more hope for Tony, from what Mrs. Brenner said, than from what she had heard from Christie.

"All right, Bailiff. Would you please bring in the complainant and defendant," said D. J., smiling knowingly at Katie. She felt all of them staring at her back as she left the room to get Tony and Mr. Bartosik.

Things didn't go as badly as Katie had thought they might for Tony. When it was all over, he had been sentenced to help Mr. Bartosik clean up the bathrooms after school for one full week. If Tony could get paid for all the work he has to do from his sentences, thought Katie, he'd be rich.

"How about I pick you up at six-thirty?" he asked.

She whispered back, "I'll be ready."

She was too nervous to eat supper, and Willie grinned sympathetically and said, "First-date jitters, huh?"

Katie nodded. "You're going to like him, Mom. He gets into trouble sometimes, but he really is a nice person. I don't know why I'm the only one who understands that."

"Well, it sounds to me as if you're able to bring out the best in him," said Willie. "Others may not understand now, but I'll bet they will eventually."

Katie thought about her mother's words as she dressed for her date. Maybe she shouldn't have waited so long to go out with him. Maybe the more she was around him, the nicer he would get and the faster everyone else would be able to see it. After all, he had gotten excited about the march for hunger almost as soon as she had mentioned it. There was only one tiny thing that bothered her about Tony, his dislike for Shawnie.

"I'm not going to mention Shawnie Pendergast one single time all evening," she vowed out loud as she brushed her hair. "And if her name comes up, I'll change the subject. I won't let anything spoil this date tonight."

At six-twenty the doorbell rang. Surprised, Katie raced down the stairs calling out, "I'll get it, Mom." It had to be Tony, she thought, but why was he getting here ten minutes early?

Katie stopped in the foyer and glanced in the mirror by the front door for one last look. Her red hair had been brushed into soft waves, and she had applied the perfect amount of lip gloss. She nodded approvingly to herself, took a deep breath, and opened the door.

She blinked in surprise when she saw that it wasn't Tony. Instead, standing there on the front porch with a suitcase in her hand, was Shawnie Pendergast.

She looked at Katie with pleading eyes. "Can I come in?" she asked. "I've run away."

Katie couldn't say anything for a moment. She just stood there, staring at Shawnie in shocked silence and trying to comprehend what she had just heard.

"You ran away?" she murmured finally. "What happened?"

Shawnie nodded. "It's a long story, but believe me, I *had* to get out of there." She took a step toward the door. "Is it okay if I come in?" she asked again. "I don't have anyplace else to go."

"Of course," said Katie. Then remembering the bruise on Shawnie's arm a few days before, she added, "Are you okay?"

Shawnie didn't answer, and just as she entered the house and set her suitcase down in the foyer, Willie called out from her office, "Honey, I'll be there in a minute to tell you good-bye. I'm on the phone."

Katie's eyes widened at the sound of her mother's voice. "It's okay, Mom," she called back. "He isn't here yet." Then she turned back to Shawnie and tried to hide an exasperated sigh. What was she going to do? Tony would be here any minute. But worse, what would her mother say if she walked out of her office and found Shawnie Pendergast standing there with her suitcase? "Come on," Katie whispered. "Let's go up to my room. Be quiet, though. I don't want Mom to hear."

Shawnie nodded and picked up her suitcase, tiptoeing up the stairs behind Katie.

"Thank you so much for letting me in. I was so scared. I've been walking around all day trying to figure out what to do." The words burst out, and her hands started trembling. "I can't go back home. Not *ever.* Can you hide me here until I figure out what to do?"

Katie bit her lower lip and tried to think. It was six twenty-nine. Tony would be here any minute. There wasn't time for Shawnie to tell her what had happened at home. And she certainly couldn't call Willie. Not until she knew more about the situation, anyway. There was only one solution.

"Do you think you can hide here in my room until I get back?" Then, seeing the puzzled look in Shawnie's eyes, she said, "I'm going to a movie with Tony Calcaterra, and he'll be here to pick me up any minute. You can't turn on a light or make any noise that Mom might hear. Okay?"

Shawnie looked at her solemnly for a minute and then nodded. "I'll be as quiet as a mouse. I promise."

"I know that's an awful thing to ask you to do," admitted Katie. "And I *hate* to fool Mom. But there's just no other way to handle it right now."

"Promise you won't tell Tony or anybody else that I'm here," Shawnie insisted. "Not *anybody.*"

"You know I won't," said Katie just as the doorbell sounded again. "That's Tony. I have to go now. Remember, don't make a sound. As soon as I get back, you can tell me what happened at home, and then we'll figure out what to do next."

"You two run along and have a good time," said Willie, and Katie could hear genuine warmth in her voice.

"Thanks, Mom," she said. "We won't be late."

"Mrs. Shannon, there's something I want to show you before we go," said Tony. He was grinning broadly.

Curiosity flashed in Katie's mind, but before she could fully wonder what he was talking about, he whirled around.

"Look at this," he said proudly, pointing to the back of his head where initials had been shaved into his close-cropped hair.

Katie gasped as she read them.

T.C.
+
K.S.

Out of the corner of her eye, she could see her mother's smile waver as she cleared her throat and said, "Oh . . . well . . . that's very nice, Tony."

"It's the latest style for boys," Katie interjected, trying to come to Tony's rescue. She didn't add that most of the boys who wore words or initials shaved into their hair were punkers or rockers and not really the type of guys she would ever go out with. She could see that her mother was still trying to comprehend Tony's bizarre haircut so she added, "Come on, Tony. We'd better get going or we'll be late."

As they left the house and got into Tony's father's

car, she turned her face away so that he could not see her exasperated expression. *Why* did he always have to blow it just when someone was starting to see how great he could be? And if he was going to shave their initials into his hair, why on earth did he have to point them out to her mother?

The drive to the movie theater was a short one, filled with polite conversation with Mr. Calcaterra. He had the same dark hair as Tony, without the initials shaved into it of course, and Katie noticed that the family resemblance was strong.

There was a crowd on the sidewalk in front of the theater, and Katie recognized most of them as being from Wacko Junior High. Mr. Calcaterra pulled into the line of cars dropping off kids, and when their turn came, Katie said, "Thanks, Mr. Calcaterra," and got out.

"Yeah, Dad, thanks," said Tony. "We'll call you to come after us later."

They were immediately engulfed in the milling crowd.

"Hi, Katie. Hi, Tony," shouted Dekeisha Adams. She and Dan Bankston were holding hands and walking toward the ticket line.

Katie waved to Dekeisha and Dan and then to Jana and Randy and Beth and Keith, who were already in line.

"Do you want to squeeze in with us?" Beth shouted.

"Just a minute. I'll ask Tony," Katie shouted back.

Just as she turned to talk to Tony, they were surrounded by a group of Tony's friends.

"Hey, Tony," shouted Bill Soliday. "Let's see that haircut."

Tony grinned and made a three-quarter turn so that everyone could see the initials shaved into the back of his hair.

"Whoa!" yelled Joel Murphy. "That's cool!" A cheer went up from the rest of the boys standing around them.

"T.C. + K.S.!" cried Mike Hershenfeld, gesturing toward Katie. "We all know who K.S. is!"

Katie felt her face turning the same shade of red as her hair. This was *not* the way she had imagined her first date would begin. "Come on, Tony. Let's get in the ticket line," she urged, tugging at his arm. Maybe when they got into the dark theater where no one would be able to see his haircut the teasing would stop.

"See you guys later," Tony called to his friends, and followed Katie to the end of the ticket line. Katie noticed that Jana and Beth and their dates had already bought tickets and disappeared into the lobby. We'll probably never be able to find them once we get inside, either, she thought.

"Well, Your Honor, you haven't said how you like my haircut," said Tony, grinning impishly. "What's the verdict?"

"To be perfectly honest, I haven't decided yet," admitted Katie. "I mean, it's better than writing it on the school walls with spray paint and having to appear before Teen Court the way you did the other time."

They both laughed at that.

"I did it so that everybody would know how much I

like you," Tony said softly. "But mostly I wanted to make sure that you got the message."

"Message received," answered Katie, feeling warm and tingly. She had to admit that Tony really did like her even though he didn't always show it in a way she would have preferred. She was trying to decide how to tell him that she liked him, too, when her attention was caught by a man and a woman walking through the crowd of teenagers and looking in all directions with anxious expressions on their faces. They were both tall and extremely well dressed. The woman had short ash-blond hair, and for an instant when she turned toward them, Katie thought she looked familiar.

"Tony Calcaterra!" the woman called out.

Looking surprised, Tony glanced toward her. "Oh, hi there, Mrs. Pendergast."

Katie was stunned. In the excitement over Tony's haircut, she had completely forgotten about Shawnie hiding at home in her bedroom. That's why the woman had looked familiar. She was tall and blond and looked a lot like Shawnie.

By this time both of Shawnie's parents had made their way through the crowd to where Tony and Katie stood.

"What are you doing at the movie on kids' night?" joked Tony. "Don't you know that they won't let you in on Friday night unless you go to Wacko Junior High?"

"We're looking for Shawnie," Mr. Pendergast said solemnly.

"She didn't come home after school, and we're worried sick," added Mrs. Pendergast.

Katie swallowed hard. They really did look worried as they scanned the crowd for sight of their daughter.

"I haven't seen her," said Tony. "Have you, Katie?"

"Katie?" asked Mrs. Pendergast. "Are you Katie Shannon?"

"Yes, ma'am," Katie answered. The blood was pounding in her temples. She didn't want to answer Tony's question. It would be awful to lie and say she hadn't seen Shawnie, but she couldn't tell on Shawnie either.

"It's nice to meet you, Katie," said Mrs. Pendergast. "Shawnie has said a lot of nice things about you."

"We've just about run out of places to look for her," said Mr. Pendergast, frowning and shaking his head. "Will you give us a call if she shows up either here or at Bumpers?"

"Tell her we're terribly worried, and we want her to come home," Mrs. Pendergast added.

"Sure thing, Mrs. P," said Tony, and Katie nodded, grateful that they hadn't asked her again if she had seen Shawnie.

As they moved on through the crowd, Katie let out a deep breath she hadn't known she was holding. She needed to talk to Shawnie and find out what was really going on. Things had happened too fast. She hadn't had time to think straight when Shawnie appeared on her doorstep because it was time for her date with

Tony. Still, she should have realized how serious the situation was.

Tony sighed. "See? I told you Shawnie was trouble. It's just like her to do something lunatic like running away."

Katie didn't answer, and for the rest of the evening she had a hard time concentrating on the things going on around her. She barely saw the movie, and even though she had fun being with Tony and they sat at a big table with her friends and their dates at Bumpers afterward, her mind kept wandering to Shawnie hiding in the dark in her room.

CHAPTER

11

*O*n the ride home from Bumpers, Tony brought up the subject that had been on Katie's mind all evening.

"I wonder if Shawnie Pendergast has gone home yet."

"Her parents certainly looked worried," said Katie, not wanting to deal with his question. Shawnie *hadn't* gone home yet unless she had climbed out of Katie's upstairs window and shinnied down the maple tree that grew beside the house, and Katie knew that wasn't very likely. What's more, she was beginning to have serious doubts about how smart it had been to let Shawnie hide there. Willie would be berserk by now if she were ever to run away like that. Didn't Shawnie care about how upset her parents were? "I hear that

Mr. and Mrs. Pendergast are awfully strict," added Katie, "and they try to buy her affection instead of letting her do the things normal kids get to do."

"They are pretty strict," Tony admitted. "And they used to come down on her pretty hard when we were in Copper Beach Elementary."

Katie wanted to ask Tony more about Shawnie and her situation at home, but Mr. Calcaterra had reached her house and was pulling up to the curb. She said good-night to Tony's father and got out of the car.

"I'll be back in a minute," Tony called to his dad as he followed Katie onto the porch.

They stopped in front of the door, and Katie felt little tingles tiptoe up her spine as Tony took her hand. "Move over this way a little," he said, tugging at her hand.

Katie chuckled. "What are you doing?" she asked as she allowed herself to be pulled along.

"Okay. Stop right here," said Tony. "This is just perfect. There's an evergreen tree between us and my dad so now he can't see us."

They were standing so close that Katie could have counted his eyelashes if the moon had been full. Suddenly Tony put his arms around her and kissed her. "I had a terrific time tonight," he said.

"So did I," said Katie.

"I'm really glad we're doing the march for hunger together, too." A grin spread over his face, and his eyes began to twinkle. "I never knew staying out of trouble could be so much fun, *Your Honor*."

Katie smiled but she didn't answer for a moment.

She wanted to say that she was glad that he was staying out of trouble, too. She also wanted to tell him that she wished she hadn't waited so long to go out with him, but standing on the dark porch with him so near suddenly made her feel shy.

"I guess I'd better go in," she finally said.

"I'll call you tomorrow about the march."

"Okay. Good night." She smiled at him to let him know she really meant what she had said.

Katie hurried into the house and then closed her eyes as she leaned against the door. "I do like Tony," she whispered to herself. "I *really* do."

"How did it go, honey?" asked Willie, who was coming into the living room from the hallway. "Did you have fun?"

Katie felt such a wide smile stretch across her face that she knew she must look like a happy-face sticker, but she couldn't help it. "We had a *terrific* time," she said. "I'll tell you all about it in the morning."

Willie smiled knowingly at Katie, and it made her blush, but she didn't care. She felt as if she were the luckiest girl in the world. They said good-night, and Katie hurried up the stairs to her room. She would have to put off her daydreams of Tony at least until in the morning. Right now she had to talk to Shawnie.

At first when she opened the door everything looked so normal and so still that it was hard to believe anyone could be hiding in her room. She tiptoed in and closed the door behind her. Light streaming in the window made her desk, her bed, even the floor look as if it were frosted with moon dust.

"Shawnie? Are you here?" she whispered, half-hoping no one would answer.

The dark smudge beside the window that was Katie's curtain grew thicker as Shawnie moved forward and then stepped into the moonlight. "Here I am," she whispered back. "I was afraid it might be your mother."

"Are you okay?" asked Katie, flipping on the light.

"Sure. But I'll have to admit I'm glad you're back. Hiding in a dark room is really spooky. I tried not to move around, but your mom came upstairs a couple of times. I thought she had heard me, and I almost died."

Katie sat down on the end of her bed, crossing her legs Indian fashion, and Shawnie sprawled across the other end, lying on her stomach and propping her chin in her hand.

"I met your mom tonight," said Katie. "And your dad, too. They were at the theater looking for you. They acted really worried."

Shawnie made a face. "You said it right when you said they *acted*. They probably convinced you, too. Believe me, someday they're going to get an Academy Award for their acting. I ought to know. I see it all the time."

"Shawnie, we have to talk," said Katie. "I didn't stop to think about how serious running away really is when I said you could hide here."

"Oh," said Shawnie, pulling herself up to a sitting position. Her expression changed from the look of anger she had worn while she talked about her parents to a combination of hurt and disbelief. She lowered her eyes sadly, tracing the patterns in the bedspread with her finger, and went on, "If you don't want me to stay overnight, just say so. I don't have anywhere else to go, but that's okay. I can just walk around all night or go to the bus station or something."

"Shawnie, you know that's not what I mean," Katie snapped. "Of course you can stay here. I just need to know why you ran away. What did your parents do to you? Did they beat you or something like that? Maybe we should call the police."

"You can't call the police!" There was panic in her voice. "Promise me you won't. Okay?"

"Will you tell me what happened at home?" Katie insisted.

Shawnie took a deep breath and let it out slowly. Katie could see tears welling in her eyes as she continued to look down and trace the patterns on the bespread. "I can't," she whispered. "Not yet. Especially not tonight. I know you can't understand. How could you?" She sighed again. "It's just too hard to talk about it right now, but maybe I'll be able to in the morning. That is . . . if I'm still here in the morning."

Katie looked helplessly around the room as if searching for the solution to this predicament and hoping to find it magically written on the walls. What was she going to do? She couldn't hide Shawnie and not tell anyone, knowing that her parents were going out of their minds with worry. It wasn't fair to them. But it would be even less fair to Shawnie to turn her out onto the street when she needed help so badly.

Shawnie got up and crossed the room to where her

suitcase sat on the floor by the dresser. As she picked it up, she turned back toward Katie. There were tears streaming down her face.

"Wait," cried Katie, rushing to her and taking the suitcase out of her hand. "I want you to stay. Honest. Everything's going to be okay. I promise."

CHAPTER

12

Katie was amazed at how complicated it was to hide Shawnie from her mother. She hated having to do it, and she also knew deep down that Willie would want to protect Shawnie and help her any way she could. It was just that Katie needed more answers from Shawnie before she brought her mother in on the situation. Otherwise, Willie might make Shawnie go home. But since Shawnie was still too upset to talk to Katie about what her parents had done, it was a cinch she wouldn't talk to Willie either. Katie had no choice but to keep Shawnie's presence a secret for now.

One of the toughest problems was going down the hall to the bathroom. Katie had never realized just how far the bathroom was from her bedroom until Shawnie needed to use it. It was also right by the top of the stairs, and Willie might come up to bed any minute and catch Shawnie sneaking through the halls.

"I'll stand guard outside the door," Katie finally said, "but you'll have to let me in if I hear her coming."

Shawnie nodded and the two girls crept down the hall. Katie was in the lead, watching the stairway and listening for sounds of her mother.

"So far, so good," she whispered as Shawnie disappeared into the bathroom, fumbled for the light switch, and closed the door.

Katie crouched at the top of the stairs and waited. Suddenly the light in the stairwell dimmed. One of the living room lamps had gone off. That meant that her mother was coming to bed. Getting down on her hands and knees, Katie peered under the banister. Willie was making her bedtime rounds, closing the living room drapes, checking the lock on the front door—all in preparation for coming upstairs.

Leaping to the bathroom door, Katie rapped softly and called as loudly as she dared, "Shawnie. Let me in."

Silence. And then the toilet flushed. Katie bit her lower lip and looked toward the stairs. Willie wasn't there yet, but she would be any second.

If I knock softly again, Shawnie won't hear over the sound of the commode, she thought. And if I yell or knock loudly, Mom will hear.

There was only one thing to do. Opening the door, Katie barged on in. Shawnie was standing by the sink. She looked at Katie in surprise, but Katie held up her hand for silence. Then she reached behind the shower curtain and turned the water on full blast.

"What are you doing?" whispered Shawnie.

"Mom's on her way up. If she thinks I'll be in here for a while, she'll probably go on to bed instead of waiting around to tell me good-night," Katie whispered back.

Shawnie nodded hopefully, and they stared silently at the bathroom door.

"Katie," Willie called from the other side. "Can I bother you to come in while your water warms up? I'll just be a minute."

The two girls exchanged wide-eyed looks of panic. Oh, no! thought Katie. Why do we have to live in a house with only one bathroom?

Thinking quickly, she shoved Shawnie toward the bathtub. "Get in," she whispered. "Hide behind the shower curtain."

"But I'll get *soaked*!" protested Shawnie.

"It's better than getting *caught*!" argued Katie. She was praying that Willie couldn't hear their voices over the sound of the shower.

"Katie? Did you hear me?"

"Yeah, Mom. Just a minute."

Katie gave Shawnie one last warning look and nudged her toward the tub again. Shawnie puckered up her face as if she were going to cry before hoisting a foot over the side of the tub and disappearing behind the curtain.

"Okay, Mom," Katie called. "You can come in now."

*   *   *

"At least you got a shower," said Katie when they were back in her room again and sharing the hair dryer.

"But my clothes are soaked," Shawnie said in a pouty voice. "And my boots. Just *look* at my *boots*."

Katie had to admit that Shawnie's gorgeous leather lace-up boots were a mess. "They'll probably look okay when they dry," she said hopefully.

Shawnie was not to be consoled. "Are you kidding? They'll be covered with water spots. And besides, you hid them in the back of your closet where air can't possibly get to them. It will take them *days* to dry completely. They'll probably *mildew*."

Katie shrugged, thinking that Shawnie's boots were the least of both of their worries right now. The next thing to be considered was the sleeping arrangements. Katie hated to put Shawnie on the floor, but she had to. It wasn't that there wasn't plenty of room in her big, double bed. It was just that tomorrow was Saturday, and sometimes Willie popped into her room on Saturday morning to tell Katie that she was going jogging or that she was heading to the grocery store to beat the weekend crowd. Actually, now that Katie thought about it, Willie was pretty unpredictable when it came to popping into her room. Sometimes she popped in to say good-night, as well. There was no doubt about it, Shawnie would have to sleep on the floor on the opposite side of the bed from the door.

Katie took half of her own covers and one of her pillows and spread them on the floor while Shawnie watched in silence. Katie wasn't sure if Shawnie was still upset over going into the shower with all her clothes on or if she didn't like the idea of sleeping on the floor. Don't be silly, Katie scolded herself. She's just run away from home. She's upset over that.

To Katie's amazement, Shawnie went to sleep as soon as her head hit the pillow. She must be exhausted, Katie decided. Determined to put Shawnie's problems out of her mind until morning, Katie turned over on her side and thought about Tony. Their date seemed as if it had happened a million years ago, and yet he had kissed her good-night a mere hour before.

She smiled to herself as she remembered the initials shaved into his hair: T.C. + K.S. Leave it to Tony, she thought tenderly. When she had first gotten to know him, it had seemed as if he were nothing more than a show-off, but now she knew that wasn't true at all. He was simply willing to take chances for things he cared about. Just the way she was taking chances for Shawnie Pendergast right now. But would he understand that if she confided in him? What would he think if he knew she was hiding Shawnie in her room?

CHAPTER

13

A banging sound at her bedroom door brought Katie out of a deep sleep. "Katie! Come downstairs quickly. There's something about Shawnie Pendergast on television."

Katie opened one eye to see Willie's head poking through the half-open door. The next instant she was wide-awake and bolting out of bed.

"Come on," Willie urged. "Shawnie's run away, and her parents will be on the morning news right after the commercial making an appeal for her to come home."

Passing her mother in the hall, Katie streaked down the stairs and skidded to a halt in front of the small television set on the kitchen counter. On the screen, a cowboy was strumming a guitar and singing a ballad

about a gentle laxative. The Pendergasts would probably be on next, she thought.

Climbing onto a stool at the end of the counter,
Katie caught her breath and shooed the cobwebs of
sleep out of her brain. The whole business about hiding Shawnie was coming back to her now, pressing
down on her like a lead weight.

"Glass of milk?" offered Willie as the commercial
ended and the camera shot went to the news desk and
the reporter who was giving the news.

Katie shook her head and leaned closer to the set to
hear what he had to say.

"Ladies and gentlemen, as we reported earlier, a local thirteen-year-old girl, Shawnie Pendergast, is missing from her home. Authorities began searching for
her yesterday afternoon when she did not return from
classes at Wakeman Junior High, and a check of atten-
dance records showed that she had not been in school
all day. At this time there is no evidence of foul play,
and both the parents and the police are proceeding on
the assumption that Shawnie Pendergast has run away
from home. Here with me now are Mr. and Mrs. Pendergast, Shawnie's parents, with an appeal to their
daughter to come home."

Katie held her breath as the camera angle widened to
include a man and a woman seated at the news desk.
She recognized them as the same two people who had
talked to Tony and her at the theater the night before.
Their faces looked haggard. They were even wearing
the same clothes they had had on at the theater, and

Katie felt a stab of guilt as she wondered if they had been up all night waiting for news of Shawnie.

Mr. Pendergast spoke first. "Shawnie, this is your father." He stopped, giving an embarrassed little laugh as if he had temporarily forgotten that she would be able to see him on the screen. "Your mother and I are very worried. Please come home. We know you are upset, but there isn't anything that we can't work out together."

He turned his head slightly and looked at Shawnie's mother, and as he did so, the camera zoomed in on her, showing tears brimming in her eyes. "Shawnie, I just want you to know . . ." Her voice broke and she looked away. When she had composed herself, she looked into the camera again and said, "I just want you to *remember* that we love you very much and we want you to come home."

"Wow!" said Katie as the camera shot swung back to the reporter who went on with the morning's news. It was all she could say. Her mind had gone numb with panic.

"Katie, you've got to think hard," said Willie, picking up her hand and looking straight into her eyes. "You're her friend. Where would Shawnie go? We've got to help find her if we can. Do you realize how dangerous it is out there for someone alone?"

Katie dropped her eyes and pulled her hand away. "I . . . I . . ." she began. "I have to go to the bathroom."

Racing up the stairs, she darted into the bathroom and sank against the door. She did not turn on the light, but in the darkness she could see the faces of

Shawnie's parents as if the television set had followed her up the stairs and into the pitch-black room. They couldn't have looked more sincere when they said they loved her. It was obvious that they were worried sick about Shawnie, and still at this very moment she was totally safe, sound asleep not more than a dozen feet away.

What am I going to do? The question kept spinning around in her brain, and yet she knew that there was one thing she had to do. She had to talk to Shawnie. She had to find out what had happened once and for all. Then she would be able to figure out what to do next.

Slipping quietly out of the bathroom so that Willie would not hear, she tiptoed to her room and shut the door behind herself. To her surprise, Shawnie was sitting in the middle of her bed in her bathrobe brushing her long blond hair.

"What was that all about?" she asked. "Did I hear your mom say that my parents were on television?"

"That's right," said Katie. "And you should have seen how worried they looked. They even have the police looking for you. You've got to tell me what happened, Shawnie. Right now."

Shawnie laughed softly. "I see they even have *you* convinced. Didn't I tell you that they were fabulous actors?" She paused and Katie started to protest, but Shawnie spoke again before Katie could get a word out. "I suppose Mom had tears in her eyes and they both said they loved me. HA! That's just to make themselves look good so they'll get all the sympathy. It worked, too. Didn't it? You look as if you're ready to turn me in."

Katie felt herself blushing, and the doubt that had burned so strongly a moment ago flickered and went out as she looked at Shawnie. Her chin was raised bravely as if daring Katie to call her parents, and she absently rubbed the bruise on her right arm, which had turned a sickly shade of yellow.

"Can't you tell me what happened?" pleaded Katie, sitting down on the bed beside her friend. "You know I want to help you. I promised you that I would. I won't go back on my word. Don't you know that?"

Shawnie nodded. "I know that, Katie. It's just that . . . well . . ." She sighed deeply. "It was awful. That's all that I can tell you right now. You've got to believe me. Oh, please, Katie. I don't know what I'd do without you."

Katie bit her lower lip and thought about Willie. There was no way she could keep Shawnie hidden from her mother very much longer. Couldn't Shawnie understand that?

Suddenly there were sounds in the hallway. .

"Katie? Did I hear voices coming from your room?" The door swung open, and Willie started in only to stop cold when she saw Shawnie sitting on the bed.

CHAPTER

14

"*S*hawnie?" Willie whispered in disbelief. "You're *here?*"

Katie jumped to her feet. She held her breath as Shawnie lowered her eyes and said quietly, "Hi, Mrs. Shannon."

"I was going to tell you." The words burst out before Katie could stop them. She looked pleadingly at her mother. "We have to help her. She says it's awful at home."

"I don't know what I would have done without Katie," said Shawnie, looking up at Katie's mother. "I didn't have anywhere to go or anyone else to turn to, and I couldn't stay at home *one minute longer.*"

Willie crossed the room and sat down on the bed,

putting her arms around Shawnie. "Of course we'll help you. We'll do whatever we can. But this is also very serious," she said. "Your parents are terribly worried, and even the police are looking for you. I think you'd better go downstairs and call your mother and father right away to let them know you're okay."

Shawnie lowered her eyes again and murmured, "I can't."

"If you don't want to talk to them yourself, I'd be glad to call them for you," offered Willie.

Shawnie shook her head. "You don't understand. Nobody understands. Everybody thinks that just because they're my parents, they're automatically right and I'm wrong. It isn't like that. You have to believe me when I tell you that I can't talk to them on the phone and I can't go home. Besides," she added, looking straight at Katie, "you promised, Katie. You said you'd do anything you could to help me, and all I ask is that you and your mom let me hide here a little while longer."

No one said anything for a moment, and Katie could feel her pulse pounding in her ears. What was Willie going to do? She couldn't believe that her mother would make Shawnie go home. Willie had always been there for people who were in trouble or needed help. It had been from watching her mother stand up for her causes that Katie had been convinced to become the same kind of person.

"I did promise I'd help her," Katie admitted.

"I have no objection to your staying here, Shawnie," said Willie. "But first, you *must* call your parents.

They're imagining all sorts of terrible things that could have happened to you."

"That's what you think," Shawnie muttered.

"Perhaps if you tell us what sort of problems you're having with your parents, we can help you work out a solution," said Willie. "There isn't any problem that can't be solved," she added with a reassuring smile.

"You wouldn't understand," Shawnie said, shaking her head again. "Nobody would. They're just so . . . so mean. They won't let me do *anything*."

"Do you mean that you ran away because they wouldn't let you do something that you wanted to do?" asked Willie.

"See!" cried Shawnie. "I knew you wouldn't understand. You think that just because they said no to something I wanted, I ran away. Well, there's more to it than that. A *lot* more."

"Then tell us about it," said Willie. "That's the only way we can help you."

"I can't. I *really, really* can't."

Willie sighed, and Katie could tell by her expression that her patience was running thin. Shawnie must have sensed it, too, because she jumped and raced to the closet, pulling out her suitcase and her wet clothes.

"Okay. I can tell that you don't want me here, so I'll go. I'll even go home. It's obvious that I'll have to anyway sooner or later. Nobody is going to help me. Just let me do it on my own," she said angrily. "That's all I ask."

Katie felt helpless as Shawnie pulled dry jeans and a sweat shirt out of the suitcase and wadded up the wet clothes and stuffed them in. "It's all right if you don't want to help me," she said.

"We do want to help you," Willie insisted. "It's just that running away isn't the answer. It only makes your problems worse. But we don't know what the right way to help you is if you won't talk to us."

Shawnie didn't answer. It was obvious to Katie that she was determined to leave rather than talk about her situation with her parents.

"We'll drive you home," offered Katie. It was the only thing she could think of to say.

"Of course we will," said Willie. "And I'll talk to your parents for you if you'd like me to."

"Thanks, but I want to do it all myself." Shawnie said firmly. "I'll go home by myself and I'll talk to my parents by myself. I'll really do it. You can trust me."

"Of course we trust you," said Willie.

Shawnie acted as if she didn't hear. Picking up her clothes, she left the room. Katie knew she was heading for the bathroom to dress.

"Mom, what are we going to do?" pleaded Katie as soon as she heard the bathroom door close. "We can't just desert her. I promised her I'd help."

"I know that, sweetheart," said Willie. "But hiding her is not necessarily helping her. Right now it seems to me that sending her back home is the best help we can give her."

"But what if she's in danger?" insisted Katie. "You saw the bruise on her arm. I'll bet they beat her. They might beat her even worse for running away."

"Has Shawnie ever told you that they beat her?"

"No," Katie admitted. "But I know she would never walk into a closet door, and that's the way she *says* she got the bruise. I think she just doesn't want to rat on her parents."

"Does that make sense to you?" asked Willie. "If things are so bad that she feels she has to run away, wouldn't she *want* people to know her parents were hurting her so that something could be done about it?"

Katie couldn't believe what her mother was saying. "You think she's making it all up, don't you?" she said incredulously. "You think Shawnie's lying."

"No, sweetheart. I just think we need to know a lot more before we start interfering and maybe doing things that could make the whole situation worse. If it will make you feel better, you can call Shawnie tonight and see how she's getting along. And I'll even promise that if we get any real evidence that Shawnie is in danger, we'll bring her here immediately."

Katie nodded. She felt better. She had known deep down that her mother wouldn't desert them although she was sure she wouldn't be able to explain that to Shawnie.

"I'm ready to go now," Shawnie said a few minutes later. She had brought her suitcase downstairs and had even had some toast and milk with Katie and Willie.

"Are you sure I can't drive you home?" Willie asked for the umpteenth time. "I would even be willing to let you off a block or two from your house, if you'd rather."

"No, thanks, Mrs. Shannon. I'll be okay. I just want to do it myself."

"I understand," said Willie. Then she gave Shawnie a hug and said, "I really do want to help you. If you ever need to talk, just let me know. The same goes if you ever need help talking to your parents. Okay?"

Shawnie nodded. "Okay, Mrs. Shannon. And thanks again."

Katie walked Shawnie to the door. "I'm sorry things didn't work out the way you wanted them to," said Katie.

"That's okay," said Shawnie. "It wasn't your fault. At least you tried."

The girls said good-bye, and as Katie watched Shawnie walk down the street and disappear around the corner, she felt as if she had let her friend down. After all, she had promised. It wasn't fair that Shawnie couldn't at least have some time away from her parents to get things sorted out. Maybe she should have begged and pleaded with her mother more, she thought. Maybe Willie would have given in and let Shawnie stay if she had only tried harder.

The rest of the day crawled by. Katie tried to clean her room in the morning, and she and Willie went to the mall for a little while in the afternoon, but her mind kept returning to Shawnie. What had her parents said when she got home? Were they mad? Or were they so glad to see her that they forgot to be mad? Fat chance, thought Katie. They'll probably punish her. Or . . . Katie couldn't let herself think about what else might happen. If only the day would pass faster so that she could call Shawnie and find out how she was.

"Turn on the television and we'll watch the evening

news while we devour this," said Willie as she set a
giant pizza box in the middle of the kitchen table.
They had decided that they didn't feel like cooking
supper, so they had stopped by their favorite pizza
place on the way home from the mall and carried out
one extra large with everything on it.

Katie pointed the remote controls toward the screen
and punched in the digits of their favorite channel just
as the news was starting. This time it was Marge Whitworth, the evening news anchor, who stared out at
them.

"Police are still baffled," she began, "by the disappearance of thirteen-year-old Shawnie Pendergast,
who has not been seen by her parents since she left for
school yesterday morning . . ."

Katie and Willie turned to each other with looks of
horror.

"But she said she would go home," Katie whispered.
"She *promised*."

CHAPTER

15

Katie and her mother stared at the television in silent disbelief as Marge Whitworth introduced Shawnie's parents for a second appeal.

"We are offering one thousand dollars to anyone who has any information on our daughter's whereabouts," Mr. Pendergast said. There were dark circles under his eyes, and Katie guessed that he still hadn't had any rest. Mrs. Pendergast looked equally tired.

They really are worried, thought Katie, no matter what Shawnie says.

A telephone number flashed on the screen, and Willie scribbled it onto the lid of the pizza box. "We'll call as soon as they've had time to get home. We have to tell them what we know," she said, sighing deeply.

Then, as if she were talking to herself, she shook her head and murmured, "I should never have trusted Shawnie to go home on her own. I should have known that she was too upset. I should have *insisted* on driving her home."

Katie felt a sudden sympathy for her mother. Willie had believed she was doing the best thing for Shawnie by sending her home. And she had trusted Shawnie, too, Katie thought, just the same as I did.

At that instant the phone rang. Katie jumped as if she had been stuck with a pin. Willie was sitting closer, so she answered.

"It's for you," she said, handing the receiver to Katie. "It's Tony."

"Did you see the news on TV?" he asked as soon as she said hello. "They still haven't found Shawnie. It doesn't surprise me a bit, though."

"Why not?" asked Katie. "Why are you always putting her down?"

"Oh, you'd have to know her to understand."

"I do know her," Katie insisted. "And I think she's nice. She has a lot of trouble at home and she needs somebody to help her."

"And Her Honor, Katie Shannon, is coming to the rescue," said Tony.

"Well, somebody has to. I even let her stay in my room last night, but she's gone now, and I don't know where she is."

"What!" shouted Tony. "You let her hide at your house? Wow, Katie. Can't you tell when you're being taken?"

Katie sucked in her breath in anger. "And I suppose getting petitions to allow boys to wear earrings to school was different? Was I being taken then, too?"

She slammed down the phone and spun around so that her mother would not see the tears jetting into her eyes. *Boys!* she thought. I should have known better than to trust Tony. He's just like all the others.

A little while later Willie called the Pendergasts and told them what she knew about Shawnie. Katie cringed as her mother described how Katie had hidden Shawnie in her room overnight, but Willie took all the responsibility herself for allowing Shawnie to leave for home on her own.

"What did they say?" asked Katie when Willie hung up.

Willie smiled sympathetically. "They said to thank you for letting her stay here last night. They said they understood why you did it. They also said that they understood why we let her leave this morning with just a promise to go home. They were very nice about the whole thing, and they said they were relieved to know that she didn't spend the night alone on the streets."

Katie felt a little bit better, but she was still worried about Shawnie. "Have they heard from anyone who knows where she is now?"

Willie shook her head. "Ours was the first call they had gotten."

The phone rang again a little while later. It was Jana this time. She had seen the telecast about Shawnie, too, and had called because she knew Katie had been so concerned about Shawnie earlier.

"I just don't know what to do," said Katie after she told Jana the whole story. "I don't know where else she would go."

"Maybe you should call some of her old friends from Copper Beach. She might have gone to one of their houses," offered Jana.

"That's a good idea, but . . ."

"But what?" asked Jana.

Katie sighed. "I don't know who her old friends are. I don't remember seeing her with anyone around school. Do you?"

"Now that you mention it, no," said Jana. "But Tony ought to know. He went to Copper Beach."

Katie bit her lower lip. She didn't want to admit that she and Tony had had a fight over Shawnie and that she had hung up on him. "I think I'll call Dekeisha instead," she said.

When she hung up from talking to Jana, she dialed Dekeisha's number, but the line was busy. She tried again a few minutes later, but it was still busy. She sat down on one of the kitchen stools and drummed her fingertips on the counter top, waiting to try Dekeisha's number again and thinking about Shawnie.

She had never paid much attention to Shawnie's other friends before, but now that she thought about it, she couldn't remember ever seeing Shawnie with anyone else. Didn't the other girls from Copper Beach like her? Were they jealous of her beautiful clothes? Or did it have something to do with the reason Tony didn't like her?

Katie jumped, startled by a sound she couldn't identify. She glanced toward the living room where Willie sat on the sofa watching television. Her mother couldn't have made the noise. And besides, Katie thought, it sounded as if it came from the basement.

Maybe it was Libber, she thought, looking around for the yellow cat. I haven't seen her all day. Maybe she went downstairs with Mom sometime and got stuck down there when the door closed.

Katie opened the door to the basement and flipped on the light switch. "Libber?" she called softly as she crept down the stairs. The basement was dark and musty, and she hated going down there after dark. It made her shiver, reminding her of the spooky stories The Fabulous Five used to tell at slumber parties when they were younger.

"Here, kitty, kitty," she called. "Come on, Libber. I'll take you back upstairs."

That's funny, she thought when Libber did not appear. Where is that cat?

She was growing accustomed to the dimness and she scanned the dark shapes of storage boxes sitting around the room for a pair of golden eyes and a long, flicking tail.

Suddenly one of the shapes moved. Katie felt a scream gathering in her throat, but before she could utter a sound, she heard someone call her name, and Shawnie stepped out of the shadows.

CHAPTER

16

*R*ushing forward, Shawnie whispered, "Shhh! Don't make any noise. *Please!*"

"How did you get in here?" Katie whispered back over the pounding of her heart. "You scared me to death. And what are you doing here, anyway? You promised you'd go home."

"I know I did," said Shawnie. Her eyes were big and pleading. "And I was going, too. But when I got around the corner, I knew I couldn't. I thought about coming back here and talking to your mom, but I knew she'd just send me home again and that this time she would see to it that I got there. I was sitting in the grass behind your house trying to decide where to go when I heard your car pull out of the driveway. I peeked around a bush and saw that you were both in it, so I tried the door on the side of the garage, and it was open. You can figure out the rest."

"You mean you've been here all day?" asked Katie. Shawnie nodded.

"And I'll bet you haven't eaten anything either. You must be starved."

Shawnie nodded again. "I almost died when I smelled pizza a little while ago. But don't worry about me. I'll be okay. The main thing is not to let your mother know I'm down here."

Katie's mind was racing. How could she *not* tell Willie that Shawnie was hiding in their basement? But Shawnie was right about one thing. If Willie knew, she would take Shawnie straight home to her parents. I have to stall while I figure out how to handle this, she thought.

"There are a couple of slices of pizza left," she said. "I'll sneak up and get them out of the fridge." Seeing panic in Shawnie's eyes, she added, "Mom will just think I ate them."

Katie managed to get the pizza slices and a can of soda out of the refrigerator without attracting Willie's attention and slipped back down to the basement. She watched Shawnie gulp down the food and thought about her predicament. Most of all she wanted to be fair. Fair to Shawnie. Fair to her mother. Even fair to Shawnie's parents since she knew they were genuinely worried. But how could she be fair to everyone? She was caught in the middle.

"Did you know that your parents are offering a one-thousand-dollar reward for information on where you are?" she asked.

Shawnie's face lit up. "They are? Cool! Maybe you can call them when I'm ready to go home, and they'll give it to you."

"Mom's already called them and told them that you were here last night," said Katie, regretting it the instant the words were out. Now Shawnie would never trust Willie again. That only made her own predicament worse.

Shawnie must have sensed Katie's helpless feeling because she moved closer and said, "I know you're trying to do the right thing. That's the kind of person you are. You're fair and you always try to help people when they need it. That's why you've got to promise that you won't give me away. I *can't* go home. All I can tell you is that I'll be in terrible danger if I do. You're the only one I could turn to who would listen or care."

Katie didn't know what to say. How could she possibly not do what Shawnie was asking when she needed help so badly? At least her parents knew she hadn't been kidnapped or anything like that. But still . . .

"Katie? Where are you, sweetheart? You have a phone call."

Katie shot to attention at the sound of Willie's voice.

"I'm in the basement . . . looking for Libber," she shouted. "I'll be up in a minute."

Turning to Shawnie, she whispered, "I have to go now. I'll try to get back down later and bring you some blankets and stuff. We'll figure out what to do in the morning."

Racing up the stairs, she shut the basement door behind her and grabbed the phone.

"Hi. It's me again," said Jana. "I was just wondering if you found out anything about Shawnie from Dekeisha."

"Not yet," said Katie. "I called twice, but her line was busy both times." She briefly considered confiding in Jana that Shawnie was in her basement but decided against it. Willie might overhear, and Katie wasn't prepared for that. "I'll try again now," she added, "and I'll let you know if I find out anything."

Katie hung up the phone a moment later and started to turn away when she changed her mind. Maybe she ought to call Dekeisha after all. It wouldn't hurt to check out a few things about Shawnie while she had the chance. This time the phone rang, and Dekeisha answered.

"Hey, I saw you at the movie with Tony Calcaterra last night," said Dekeisha after the two girls had exchanged hellos. "I thought you two would start dating sooner or later."

"Right," said Katie. "Tony and I did go out last night, but it's Shawnie Pendergast that I'm calling about."

"Oh, so you finally found out about that, huh?"

Katie frowned at the receiver. "What are you talking about? What did I finally find out about?"

"That Tony used to be Shawnie's boyfriend in Copper Beach, but she dumped him. Hey, wait a minute. Did I spill something?"

Katie was flabbergasted. "Oh, no. I knew all about

that," she lied. "I've got to go now. My mom's calling. Bye."

She felt like a zombie as she headed for her room. Tony had been the boyfriend Shawnie had mentioned the day she went to Bumpers with The Fabulous Five, and *she* had dumped *him*. So that was it. No wonder Tony didn't like her anymore, and it was also no wonder that he always put her down. He was still mad, and he was trying to turn everyone against her.

"And I almost believed him," Katie whispered under her breath. "I almost let him convince me that I couldn't trust Shawnie when he was the one with the problem."

Katie gathered up the blankets and the pillow that Shawnie had used the night before and put them in the chair beside her bedroom door. She would wait until her mother went to bed, and then she would take them down to the basement for Shawnie to use tonight and any other night she needed them. She would take some food down, too, and a flashlight and maybe her portable radio if Shawnie would promise to keep the volume turned down low.

Poor Shawnie, she thought. Everyone is against her. I really *am* the only one she has to turn to. No matter what, I won't let her down.

CHAPTER

17

*T*he next day, Sunday, was one of the most frantic days of Katie's entire life. Whenever Willie's back was turned, she raced to the basement loaded down with whatever supplies she could find to make Shawnie more comfortable. She took down peanut butter and jelly sandwiches, chips, a package of Oreo cookies, and once she spotted the picnic cooler stored on a shelf at the back of the basement, she sneaked down trays of ice. Then, when the ice was in the cooler, she hauled soda and a half carton of chocolate chip ice cream from the kitchen.

Shawnie had been busy, too. She had rearranged the storage boxes in one corner of the basement into the shape of a small room, using a low box as a table beside her bedding. On the table were the flashlight and radio. She had even set up two folding lawn chairs that had been stored in the basement for the winter.

"When you were younger, did you ever read the books about The Borrowers?" she asked Katie as the two sat in the lawn chairs pulling apart cookies and licking the frosting from the middle after Willie had gone out to an afternoon bridge game.

"Do you mean those tiny little people who lived in some regular-size people's house and borrowed things to furnish their own teeny tiny rooms?"

Shawnie nodded and laughed. "That's exactly how I feel, like one of The Borrowers. The only difference is that I'm regular size, too."

Katie tried to laugh with her, but she couldn't. "Are you okay down here?" she asked. "I mean, it can't be very comfortable."

"It's just perfect. You know, there are lots of ways to be comfortable, and this is definitely more comfortable than being at home."

As Katie's sympathy for Shawnie grew, so did her admiration, and she was determined to make life in the basement as painless as she possibly could. While Willie was gone, she let Shawnie come upstairs to take a shower and wash her hair. Shawnie read the comics and the front-page story about her disappearance in the Sunday paper and was playing with Libber in the middle of the living room floor when Katie heard her mother's car pull into the driveway.

"You'd better get downstairs," she cautioned Shawnie. "Mom's back."

Shawnie scurried down the stairs, and Katie made a quick check to be sure everything was back to normal in the house before her mother came in. She wasn't able to go down to the basement again before bedtime, and she lay awake for a long time wondering if Shawnie was really as comfortable down there as she had said.

She wasn't able to see Shawnie before she left for school the next morning either, and although Shawnie had been on her mind constantly all weekend, she was amazed at how many students were talking about her on the school ground.

Alexis Duvall and Lisa Snow were the first to stop her. "Katie, did you hear about Shawnie Pendergast?" asked Alexis. "She ran away from home. Isn't that awful?"

Katie nodded and kept on walking toward The Fabulous Five, who stood by the fence. She had wanted to mention to Alexis that maybe staying home would have been even worse for Shawnie than running away, but she hadn't. It wouldn't do any good. Nobody else really cared about Shawnie but her.

"Did you ever talk to Dekeisha?" asked Jana as soon as Katie reached the group of friends.

"Not really," said Katie. She didn't want to mention her conversation with Dekeisha about Tony.

"What was that all about?" asked Melanie. "Does Dekeisha know where Shawnie is?"

"No," said Jana. "At least we don't think so. Katie was going to ask her about Shawnie's friends from

Copper Beach. Neither of us can remember ever seeing her going around with anyone."

"Gee, me either," said Beth. "Whenever I noticed her, she was by herself until she got to be friends with Katie."

"That doesn't mean she doesn't have friends," snapped Katie.

"But if we knew who they were, we might know where she is," insisted Jana. "Especially since she went to Katie first."

Christie, Melanie, and Beth all looked at Katie in surprise, so she told them about Shawnie's hiding in her room on Friday night and then promising to go home Saturday morning. As badly as she wanted to ask her best friends' help, she knew she had to keep it a secret where Shawnie was hiding now.

"Maybe Mandy McDermott would know," said Christie. "She's in my social studies class and she went to Copper Beach. I'll ask her."

When Katie went to her locker just before the bell, Tony was waiting for her. Even with all the excitement over Shawnie, he had been in her mind. At first she had simply been angry at him for deceiving her about Shawnie and making her think that there was something wrong with her new friend. But now she felt terribly sad because she had liked him so much and had been so convinced that he was special. Well, he isn't, she told herself firmly. He's nothing but a macho show-off.

"Good morning, Your Honor," Tony said sarcastically.

"Morning," she muttered.

"Don't forget that march for hunger is this Saturday and that we still have a lot of work to do on it," he went on. "We need to have sign-up sheets in the cafeteria again, and a few posters around town wouldn't hurt either."

The sarcasm was gone from his voice, but so was the twinkle that usually showed in his eyes when he talked to her. It was obvious to Katie that he was as upset with her as she was with him.

"Okay," she said tersely. "I'll see you at lunch." Jerking open her locker, she got out her books, slammed it shut, and left him standing there.

She had taken only a few steps down the hall when she stopped and glanced back over her shoulder. Tony was still standing beside her locker solemnly watching her walk away. She bit her lower lip and tried to decide what to do. A small worry was beginning to burrow into her mind the way Libber sometimes burrowed into her lap. Libber would poke and nudge until she fit the contours perfectly, and then she would settle down, taking complete possession of Katie's lap so that she was almost impossible to dislodge. Katie knew she would have trouble dislodging this troublesome thought, too, unless she faced it head-on. After all, she reasoned, there was a strong possibility that she was the one being unfair this time. Maybe she was jumping to conclusions. Even if it was true that Shawnie had dumped Tony back in Copper Beach Elementary, that didn't automatically mean that it was all his fault.

She turned around slowly, meaning to return to her locker and to Tony, but she had waited too long. He was gone.

The morning did not get better. Christie stopped her in the hallway while classes were passing between first and second period.

"I talked to Mandy," said Christie, "and you won't believe what she said."

"What?" asked Katie.

"She said that Shawnie doesn't have many friends at all. She said it was because Shawnie is a spoiled brat and she uses people to get what she wants."

Anger flashed in Katie's brain. "What did Shawnie ever do to Mandy?" she snapped. Then, seeing that her outburst had caused students to stop in the hall and stare at her, she thanked Christie and went on to her class. Still, she couldn't help wondering why everybody was picking on Shawnie.

At lunchtime Katie shared the sign-up table in the cafeteria with Tony. She wanted so badly to talk to him, to ask him what had really happened between him and Shawnie, but she didn't know how. He practically ignored her, busily shuffling the sign-up sheets whenever she looked at him.

I don't care, she told herself stubbornly. I don't want to talk to a macho, show-off *jerk* anyway.

The instant that thought had formed in her mind, she knew it wasn't true. He was macho, and he did like to show off. But he wasn't a jerk. She was the jerk for hanging up on him. She couldn't blame him for being angry. Over and over she practiced mentally what to say to him, but every time she thought she had the speech just right, more students came up to sign the lists. Finally lunch period as over, and Tony left the cafeteria without a word.

Katie avoided Bumpers after school and went straight home. Willie was hard at work at her computer, so after a fast hello to her mother, Katie slipped downstairs to check on Shawnie.

"Hi," Shawnie said brightly. "Did I miss anything major at school today?"

"No," Katie assured her. "Just the same old stuff."

"I got lucky," Shawnie bragged. "I heard your mom make a phone call to set up an interview and then go out, so I got to go upstairs and watch soap operas for almost two hours."

"That's good," Katie said halfheartedly. She knew that she should be glad that Shawnie hadn't been stuck in the dark basement all day without even a bathroom, but she felt depressed instead. Shawnie seemed incredibly happy, living in a dark basement and laughing over each report of her parents' misery. Nothing else was going right for Katie, either, and as badly as she hated to admit it even to herself, it was all because of Shawnie. No matter how hard she tried not to doubt Shawnie's word, things were beginning to stack up against her. Who really was telling the truth, anyway? Shawnie? Or Tony and Mandy and even Mr. and Mrs. Pendergast?

"I stopped by the Burger Barn and got you a hamburger and fries," said Katie after a while, pulling the bag of food out of her backpack. "I'll try to come back down before I go to bed, but I can't promise."

"Sure," said Shawnie. "I understand."

Katie dreaded hearing the evening news broadcast. She even considered asking her mother if they could skip watching it just this once. Still, she couldn't help wondering if the Pendergasts would be on again tonight. Surely they would be since Shawnie still hadn't gone home. She frowned, thinking about how unfair it was to Shawnie's parents not to know that she was okay.

When Marge Whitworth's grim face appeared on the screen a little while later, Katie knew her prediction had been right.

"Ladies and gentlemen, the parents of missing thirteen-year-old Shawnie Pendergast are here with me again to appeal once more to their missing daughter to come home."

Katie squirmed in her chair as the now-familiar pair came into focus.

"Shawnie," Mr. Pendergast began, "if you can hear my voice, please believe me when I say that your mother and I continue to worry about your safety. Further, we have decided to permit you to join the march for hunger this Saturday instead of keeping the other plans we had made, and we will donate the one-thousand-dollar reward money to the march if you will only come home."

"The *march*?" Katie whispered to herself. It was too incredible to be true. Had Shawnie really run away from home just because her parents had made other plans and wouldn't let her join the march for hunger? She had to find out right now. She jumped up from the kitchen table, and raced for the basement door.

CHAPTER

18

"Shawnie!" Katie shouted, throwing open the basement door and flipping on the light. She heard her mother gasp behind her, but she didn't care. "Shawnie, where are you? I have to talk to you."

Katie thundered down the stairs and hurried to Shawnie's corner room, sidestepping boxes that had been shoved aside to clear out space for the hideaway.

Shawnie was sitting in a lawn chair listening to Katie's radio through the headphones. But the basement light's flashing on had apparently startled her, because by the time Katie reached her, there was panic on her face.

"What's the matter?" she cried, pulling off the headphones and jumping to her feet.

Katie stopped and looked hard at Shawnie. Willie stepped up beside her, and Shawnie's eyes shifted frantically back and forth between them as if she couldn't decide whom to fear the most. Katie didn't look at her mother. She would deal with Willie's disapproval later, and she knew that her mother would be upset to find Shawnie here after sending her home once before.

"Is something wrong?" Shawnie asked softly.

Katie ignored the question. She had a question of her own. "Is it true that the reason you ran away is because your parents wouldn't let you join the march for hunger?"

"Yes," Shawnie answered, and shrugged, and then she added quickly, "But there's more to it than that."

"Like what?" demanded Katie.

Shawnie gave a deflated sign and sank back down into the chair. She sat there a moment, staring at a crack in the floor as if she were choosing her words carefully. "You see, my mom and dad are almost never home. They're both attorneys, and they have these big careers going. They're never *ever* home after school, and most of the time at least one of them misses dinner. They work a lot on Saturdays, too. They think it's terrific because they can buy lots of stuff and my college education is already paid for. I think it's the pits."

Shawnie glanced up for the first time and sighed heavily again.

"Go on, honey," Willie urged. "Tell us the rest of the story."

Shawnie nodded. "Everybody thinks I'm spoiled rotten because I have so many great clothes, but the truth is, I'd rather have my parents around once in a while than all these clothes."

"But what does that have to do with them not letting you do things?" asked Katie.

"Well, you see, making me come straight home from school every day is their way of knowing I'm safe and out of trouble. They call and check on me a lot. And since they aren't available to drive me to things, they don't have to worry about that either. It makes them feel better if I don't get involved. It's just their way of handling the situation. They're afraid something terrible will happen to me. I think it's really cool how they've been sitting at home by the phone ever since I ran away waiting for me to call. This is the longest they've been at home in years."

"But Shawnie . . ." Katie began. She felt so sorry for her friend for having parents who wouldn't let her do things and left her alone all the time, but the anger at being deceived that she had felt just a moment before had turned to confusion. That still didn't make it right to run away.

"What about the bruise on your arm?" Katie challenged. "Did you really run into the closet door, or . . . did your parents hit you?"

"I really ran into the closet door," Shawnie whispered. "I knew what you were thinking, and I guess I just let you think it."

Willie frowned thoughtfully. "Your parents were on television again a few moments ago, and they said they would cancel the plans they had made so that you could join the march for hunger if you would just go home. What plans were they talking about?"

"We were going to go away for the weekend," Shawnie huffed. "They thought it was such a big deal to plan a weekend trip since they're gone so much, but why did it have to be the same weekend as the march for hunger? I tried to explain that everybody from Wakeman would be marching and that what I really wanted was to march, too. But do you think they'd listen? No. I begged and screamed, but they kept on insisting that we should go away. They're always doing things like that. You understand, don't you?"

She looked pleadingly first at Katie and then at Willie and then back at Katie again. "They were being so *unfair*," she insisted. "You're always talking about fairness, Katie. That's why I turned to you. I knew you'd understand. And you did. Remember that you're the one who came up with the idea to invite me over and tell my mother that we were working on a project."

"I do understand," said Katie. "And I agree that they've been awfully unfair to you." She paused, thinking that Tony and Mandy and the other kids from Copper Beach had judged her unfairly, too, because they didn't understand what she was going through at home. "But you're being unfair by scaring them so badly. In fact"—she paused again, trying to find a way to express how she felt—"everyone's been unfair, and that's a shame, but I think you've been the most unfair of all."

Tears brimmed in Shawnie's eyes, and she looked quickly at Willie as if searching for support.

"I agree with Katie," said Willie. "But you can start to make things better at home by going upstairs right now and calling your parents to tell them you're okay. Then when you get home, sit down and have a long, *calm* talk with them about how you feel. It's the only way you'll ever make things better."

"No!" Shawnie shouted angrily, jumping to her feet. "And you can't make me. I'll stay down here until I . . . I . . . *mildew*!"

Katie was astounded when her mother turned to go upstairs, saying, "Okay. If that's the way you feel, then I guess there's nothing we can do. Come on upstairs, Katie. Let's finish our dinner."

Katie followed Willie up the stairs, but she couldn't understand what was going on. "We can't just leave her down there forever," she insisted. "Especially since she was right about one thing. It was partly my fault. I'll bet that I even encouraged her not to go home by talking about fairness so much."

"Maybe so," said Willie, "but she still has to stop blaming everybody else and take some responsibility herself. That's the only way she's ever going to change things. You'll have to admit, she is a little bit spoiled. But don't worry about her right now. After she thinks things over, she'll come around."

Willie paused for a moment. Her face clouded. "But as for you, young lady, you are always taking about justice. How could you possibly take justice into your own hands, hiding Shawnie and helping keep her parents in anguish without bothering to find out the whole story? Right or wrong, don't you believe that the Pendergasts had a right to know that Shawnie was okay?"

Katie tried to protest, but Willie held up her hand for silence.

"You not only jumped to the conclusion that Shawnie was the only one being treated unfairly, but then you took it into your own hands to decide that Shawnie had the right to hide out even though the police are looking for her and her parents are crazy with worry. Is that your definition of fairness?"

Katie stared, unblinking, at Willie. Half of her wanted to shout that she had only tried to help a friend when nobody else wanted to, and the other half of her felt overwhelmed by how complicated right and wrong could sometimes be. It seemed so much simpler in Teen Court when all you had to do was listen to both sides and then decide who was right or wrong. Except that it hadn't always seemed simple then either. And her mother was right, this time she hadn't even listened to both sides. How could I have forgotten such an important thing as that? she wondered.

Sighing, Katie looked at Willie. Her mother was looking at her closely, and Katie knew Willie could almost read her thoughts by watching the expression on her face. Still, she wanted to say the words out loud.

"I guess you're right," she admitted. "It was just so easy to believe Shawnie that I forgot all about what being fair really means."

Willie put her arms around Katie. "You were trying to be a good friend, and that's okay as long as it doesn't hurt anyone else."

Just then footsteps sounded on the basement steps. "Is it all right if I use the phone?" Shawnie asked sheepishly as she stepped into the kitchen. "I want to call my parents to come and get me."

After Shawnie's parents picked her up, Katie dialed Tony's number. She leaned against the wall and listened to the ringing on the other end. Five . . . six—it looked as if no one was home. Just as she was about to hang up, she heard someone answer.

"Hello." It was him.

"Hi," Katie said in a soft voice. "It's me."

She noticed the short pause before he said, "What's up, Your Honor?"

"I need to talk to you, Tony. In fact, I think I owe you an apology."

"Oh?" His voice was softer.

Katie told him the whole story about thinking that no one understood Shawnie and that her parents mistreated her and how she had helped Shawnie hide from her parents. She told him about how she finally found out the truth and knew now that everyone had been a little unfair, especially Shawnie.

"And I was unfair, too," she said. "Especially to you. I really thought you were mad at Shawnie for dumping you at Copper Beach Elementary."

"She didn't dump me at Copper Beach."

Katie was stunned. "That's what everyone says."

"I don't care what everyone says," he responded. "You ought to know that by now. That's why I didn't say anything when she told people she had dumped me. If it made her feel better, that's okay."

Katie heard him take a deep breath on the other end of the line and then he continued, "I didn't see how it would do any harm to let people think whatever she told them. I guess it has, though. It made you mad at me. I liked Shawnie a lot. I really did. But then I realized how spoiled she was, always having to get her own way, and I stopped seeing her."

Katie stared at the phone in amazement. Tony had suspected all along that Shawnie was trying to pull something. He had tried to warn Katie that she was being taken without actually putting Shawnie down, but she had been too headstrong to listen. Instead she had blamed Tony for being macho and trying to hurt Shawnie. Thank goodness she had finally decided to talk to him and straighten things out.

"Tony, I'm so sorry," she said. "I don't know how I could have doubted you."

He chuckled. "Just remember that the next time I come before Teen Court, Your Honor."

Saturday was a beautiful fall day, and crowds of people lined the three-mile course through downtown that Katie and Tony had laid out.

"I can't believe so many people turned out to support us," she said to Tony as they checked Wacko students off the registration forms and gave them badges shaped like cans of soup to pin on their shirts. They had spent Friday evening at her kitchen table drawing and cutting out the badges as if their argument had never happened.

Tony looked at his watch. "It's almost time to start the march," he said. "Is everybody here?"

"Almost," said Katie, running a pencil down the list of names. The rest of The Fabulous Five had been the first to arrive. The Wacko football team had come together, and all of the cheerleaders were here. Even Taffy Sinclair was near the front of the marchers in a new lavender jogging suit.

"Why don't we go ahead and start?" asked Tony. "Everybody's getting antsy."

Katie bit her lower lip. "Let's wait just five more minutes," she said. She didn't want to admit it out loud, but she was hoping as hard as she could that she hadn't been deceived again. If she had been, it would be absolutely the last straw.

The minutes ticked by.

"Who are we waiting for?" Tony asked impatiently after he and Katie had taken their places at the head of the crowd, and Katie was still stalling. "Come on. Let's get going."

Katie sighed. There wasn't any use waiting. They might as well get the march started.

Just then a long black limousine came streaking up the street and stopped beside the marchers. The door opened and out popped Shawnie.

"I'm here!" she shouted. "I get to march!"

Before Katie could say a word, the door on the driver's side of the car opened and Mr. Pendergast stepped out onto the street. He headed straight to Katie and handed her a folded paper.

"And here's my pledge for one thousand dollars to the march for hunger just as I promised on television," he said, smiling kindly.

A moment later the marchers were off, laughing and talking and waving to the crowd. Katie could see Willie at the edge of the sidewalk on one street they passed, and she felt so proud she almost burst. Everything had worked out perfectly. Shawnie had gone home and was making progress talking with her parents. The march was going to be a huge success, and her mother would have a terrific story to write for the paper.

"Well, Your Honor," Tony said, taking her hand as they sauntered along. "Now that you've saved Shawnie Pendergast from a fate worse than death and raised money to feed the hungry, what causes are you going to take up next?"

"Oh . . . I don't know yet," she said, tingling all over with happiness. "*We'll* think of something."

CHAPTER

19

"You're kind of quiet," Jon said as he and Christie turned the corner onto her street.

"Oh, I've just been thinking about the Super Quiz team. It sounds as if it will be a lot of fun. I just hope I can be in the matches."

"Don't worry. You're smarter than the others."

"That's easy for you to say," she responded. "But Curtis, Whitney, and Melissa aren't dummies."

"Neither are you," Jon said, putting his arm around her.

Christie jumped at his touch, then grabbed her books, pretending she had almost dropped them to cover up her nervousness from Jon. She had seen the Wakeman-Trumbull Super Quiz match the year before when she was still at Mark Twain Elementary. It was like a TV game show with two teams of students being asked questions by a moderator. If you thought you knew the answer, you slapped a button and a buzzer sounded and a light flashed. It was exciting with the kids trying to beat each other to the button, jumping up and down, and yelling and laughing.

The names of the Wakeman seventh-, eighth-, and ninth-graders who had been picked for the team this year had been announced over the school public address system that afternoon. She was proud to have been chosen, but it didn't mean she would actually get to be in the matches against other schools. She could end up being a second-stringer and never actually get to play against another school. Only two of the four people from each grade would get to participate each time.

Her thoughts came back to Jon, and she squeezed his arm. She was sorry she had jumped when he touched her. It wasn't only that she was nervous about the Super Quiz tryouts. Lately she was beginning to think she needed more space. She didn't want to have to worry about hurting his feelings every time she wanted to do something with someone else or spoke to another boy. And Jon and she had different interests.

Jon was fun to be with most of the time, but he was always there. She really wished they were best friends instead of going steady. But how could she tell him that? The thought of it made her shiver. She didn't want to hurt him, but sometime, somehow, she was going to have to talk to him about it.

And who would believe they were just friends? The kids at school thought that if you walked down the hall with a guy or went to Bumpers with him, you had to be going steady.

Christie is faced with all these problems and more, much more, in *The Fabulous Five #9: The Boyfriend Dilemma*.

ABOUT THE AUTHOR

Betsy Haynes, the daughter of a former newswoman, began scribbling poetry and short stories as soon as she learned to write. A serious writing career, however, had to wait until after her marriage and the arrival of her two children. But that early practice must have paid off, for within three months Mrs. Haynes had sold her first story. In addition to a number of magazine short stories and the Taffy Sinclair series, Mrs. Haynes is also the author of *The Great Mom Swap* and its sequel, *The Great Boyfriend Trap.* She lives in Colleyville, Texas, with her children and husband, who is also an author.

Great FREE offer
just for you!

Join SNEAK PEEKS™!

Do you want to know what's new before anyone else? Do you like to read great books about girls just like you? If you do, then you won't want to miss SNEAK PEEKS™! Be the first of your friends to know what's hot ... When you join SNEAK PEEKS™, we'll send you FREE inside information in the mail about the latest books ... *before they're published!* Plus updates on your favorite series, authors, and exciting new stories filled with friendship and fun ... adventure and mystery ... girlfriends and boyfriends.

It's easy to be a member of SNEAK PEEKS™. Just fill out the coupon below ... and get ready for fun! It's FREE! Don't delay—sign up today!

☐ **TAFFY SINCLAIR AND THE**   **15494/$2.50**
   ROMANCE MACHINE DISASTER
   by Betsy Haynes
   Taffy Sinclair is furious. Her rival, Jana Morgan, has a date with
   Randy Kirwan, the most popular boy at school. When their teacher
   conducts a computer match-up game, Jana and 9 other girls, including
   Taffy turn out to be just right for Randy. Jana vows to win him! But is
   she any match for Taffy?

☐ **THE AGAINST TAFFY**   **15712/$2.75**
   SINCLAIR CLUB
   by Betsy Haynes
   It was bad enough when Taffy Sinclair was just a pretty face. But now
   she's gone and developed a figure! This calls for drastic measures
   from the Against Taffy Sinclair Club made up of Jana Morgan and her
   four fifth-grade friends.

☐ **TAFFY SINCLAIR**   **15645/$2.75**
   STRIKES AGAIN
   by Betsy Haynes
   It is time gorgeous Taffy Sinclair had a little competition. That's what
   Jana and her friends decide to give her when they form a club called
   The Fabulous Five. But when the club's third meeting ends in disaster,
   Jana finds she has four new enemies!

☐ **TAFFY SINCLAIR,**   **15647/$2.75**
   QUEEN OF THE SOAPS
   by Betsy Haynes
   What could be worse? The snooty but perfectly gorgeous Taffy has
   done it again—she's won a part in a soap opera to play a beautiful girl on
   her deathbed. Nothing like this ever happens to Jana Morgan or her
   friends, and they're not going to stand being upstaged one more time!